THE WRONG SIDE OF REVELRY

A Novel

JEFFRY A. HEAD

The Wrong Side of Revelry: A Novel

Copyright © 2024 Jeffry A. Head

Published in the United States of America.

Cover and Interior Designed by Siori Kitajima, PatternBased.com

Cataloging-in-Publication data for this book is available from the Library of Congress

ISBN-13
eBook: 978-1-958861-25-7
Paperback: 978-1-958861-26-4

Published by The Sager Group LLC
(TheSagerGroup.net)

THE WRONG SIDE OF REVELRY

A Novel

JEFFRY A. HEAD

More Books from
The Sager Group

The Swamp: Deceit and Corruption in the CIA
An Elizabeth Petrov Thriller (Book 1)
by Jeff Grant

Chains of Nobility: Brotherhood of the Mamluks (Books 1-3)
by Brad Graft

Meeting Mozart: A Novel Drawn from the Secret Diaries of Lorenzo
Da Ponte
by Howard Jay Smith

Death Came Swiftly: A Novel About the Tay Bridge Disaster of 1879
by Bill Abrams

A Boy and His Dog in Hell: And Other Stories
by Mike Sager

Reunion in Paradise: A Novel
by L.W. Harris

The Orphan's Daughter: A Novel
by Jan Cherubin

Lifeboat No. 8: Surviving the Titanic
by Elizabeth Kaye

Into the River of Angels: A Novel
by George R. Wolfe

The Dreyfus Collection: A Novel
by Estelle Rubin Brager

See our entire library at TheSagerGroup.net

The Japanese say every person has three faces:

The first face is the face you show to the world.

*The second face is the face you show to your friends
and family.*

*The third face is the face you never show anyone —
the truest reflection of who you are.*

Acknowledgements

I wrote this book with the help and inspiration of two friends from my childhood, Alisa Harris Kesten and Russell Boston. Alisa, I knew from kindergarten; Russell, from the third grade. We grew up in Cartersville, Georgia and attended public school through twelfth grade. Off to college we went, and have led very different lives over the many years since leaving THE 'VILLE. We stayed in touch, sometimes more than others. Today we share emails daily on all things of interest, with a good deal of humor mixed in. Both my friends are very much into the political scene, for which I have no stomach. I wanted to write a crime fiction thriller that might cause some to consider things from a different angle, while being a page turner with a darn good story. Readers will determine if I succeeded. Regardless, I would not have produced the tale here told without the input from THE VIC, my acronym for THE 'VILLE INTELLECTUAL COMMITTEE. Alisa and Russell are members in good standing, and read my manuscript daily, almost in real time. Their comments were honest and mostly spot on. Alisa then edited it, doing a fabulous job. I hope you enjoy the book half as much as I enjoy my friends. N.B.: A special thank you to Leeann Kearney who, at Mardi Gras 2023, said to me, "You should write a book with a murder in the middle of a Mardi Gras ball."

One

The coke held Jenna in its edgy embrace, swaddling her in a prickly sort of love. God, she loved being a Dupreaux (Dew-pray). Actually, what she really loved was being *herself*. Ten minutes earlier, in the ladies' room, she had done a bump just to focus her for this mission. She thought of it as a mission, a surgical strike against an enemy. She had every right: by birth, money, and social standing. How could she not be the Queen of Mardi Gras, exalted by all? Yet here she was, another maiden in the New Orleans Mardi Gras court. It was a fucking outrage is what it was. That bitch Alisha Bondurant had her spot, reigning as queen and soaking up the spotlight. It enraged her. Christ, little Miss Goody Two-shoes waving and smiling, above her in the social pecking order. She nearly lost control as she rode the coke, wanting to scratch the bitch's eyes out right in the middle of the ball. She forced herself to breathe deeply for several minutes, regaining her composure. A moment of fear gripped her. Had her facial expression betrayed the absolute malice she was feeling? Did others around her see the seething hatred? Would they remember a deranged look in the interviews with cops that were certain to follow? She looked around quickly, concluding that those close to her were either too drunk or lost in the festivities to notice. Thank goodness; she was back in control, icy cool, her thoughts unseen. It was time to act, to end this bitch's reign permanently. The vengeance she held inside for years would be unleashed, and nothing would ever be the same.

The ring was not terribly remarkable. Lovely, to be sure, but simple and elegant. Far from gaudy and nouveau, not something that would be remembered later. It was a 14-karat gold band, the infinity symbol entwined around the band in a never-ending march. The stone was a gorgeous cat's-eye white opal, set horizontally from east to west. The stone was 4 carats, large enough without appearing extravagant. It belonged to her grandmother Kitty, having been in the Dupreaux family for over one hundred years. Ahh, but the best part was unseen. A small compartment hollowed out in the gold base atop which the stone sat. It was Civil War era, meant to hold a pinch of snuff. Tonight it held something much more powerful: a small fentanyl pill.

Jenna moved closer to her prey, smiling brightly for all the world to see. She kissed a couple of friends on the cheek, squeezed an arm, and worked in close to Alisha, who was beautiful and vibrant, dressed in an ivory silk lamé gown with chevrons and gold beading. She looked for cameras. They were a problem. She did not want to be in a photograph taken right before the event. Seeing none, she decided the moment was right. Alisha was embracing Taylor Brinson, one of the knights, whispering in his ear. Her arms draped casually over his shoulders, her drink open and exposed. Jenna Dupreaux deftly opened the compartment in her ring with a fingernail, exposing the small white pill. She reached as if to squeeze the hand of Alisha, tipping the pill into Alisha's drink and continuing merrily along the way. She did not stop until she was clear across the large auditorium floor, making her way to the bar for a bracing drink. She felt exhilaration, her heart pounding loudly in her chest. She feared others would hear its thump-thump, but realized it was only a little paranoia from the coke. The booze would handle that, mellowing her out.

She had just gotten her drink and turned to the room when the crowd began to stir. Hundreds of bodies blocked her view, but something was happening. A buzz was rippling through the crowd. Feigning curiosity, she asked old man

Russell what the commotion was. She gave him a thousand watt smile, knowing that the old lecher would remember her being at his side later. She leaned in, putting a boob on his arm for good measure. She thought he might faint with delight, but he shrugged and said, "No idea." Across the room the Queen of Carnival had collapsed, drink spilling. It stained the beautiful ball gown she wore. A number of prominent doctors were in the crowd, but she was gone in a flash. No amount of assistance could help Alisha. She died quickly even as the spotlights danced around the auditorium floor.

Two

The news swept the room like a wildfire jumping from tree to tree. Jenna remained in place, firmly attached to George Russell's arm. It was great cover. Her body quivered like a tuning fork. She was not sure she could have remained upright without the support. She wondered if old man Russell felt it. She was excited, sexually and emotionally. The coke helped carry her along in an almost orgasmic state. Within a couple minutes Lois Bradbury hustled over. Breathlessly she squawked, "The Queen, Alisha, just collapsed. Paramedics rushed her out. Talk is alcohol poisoning. I don't want to gossip, but you young people drink far too much during Mardi Gras." Her comment was obviously directed at Jenna.

Putting on her best look of horror, Jenna responded, "Oh, no. Not sweet Alisha. She hardly drinks." Jenna burst into tears, a talent she had cultivated over her twenty-two years on earth. She was quite good at it and found that girls got a pass when the tears flowed. George Russell whipped out his handkerchief and offered it up. Jenna gratefully accepted and hid her face from view. She could hardly contain her glee, but knew she had to keep up the act. Jeez, she was hot. She needed sexual release in the worst possible way. It occurred to her that this must be like the boys having blue balls. She would scratch her itch before the night ended.

The ball wore on for a while, but people left early. It was like a balloon deflating, they leaked out into the night. Jenna grabbed Ross, her knight, and pleaded her case for an early evening. Ross was a sweet boy, not too bright but handsome. To Jenna, he was a huge bore. As soon as Ross dropped her at her condominium she changed into a thong and tank top. She pulled on a pair of spandex Skims sculpted shorts and five minutes later hustled out to her Audi. She raced over to Dare's house and used her key to slip inside. She found him in bed. Peeling off her clothes, she yanked the sheet back and straddled him. She rubbed herself on him and soon got the response she sought. She mounted him and thrust violently up and down, culminating in their mutual release. She lay panting on his chest, never having said a word but as contented as she had been in years.

Three

Taylor Brinson sat numbly on the floor, his tailcoat sprawled awkwardly. He was an observer, mentally detached from the chaotic scene. Only a minute before, he had stood with Alisha whispering in his ear. Her arms over his shoulders, he was laughing at her commentary on the pomposity of the ball. Now she lay on the floor, spilt whiskey and crumpled napkins scattered about, Dr. May furiously compressing her chest in an attempt to revive her. Other doctors hovered around, women gasping and crying. Taylor felt cold, detached, almost as if he was in a tunnel. He knew it was bad. Her color was gone, the radiance that had defined her absent. He could hear cell phone conversations, someone screaming for paramedics. Suddenly, he realized that Dr. May was yelling at him, asking him what had happened. He had no response. She was in his ear one moment, and the next she was gasping for air as she collapsed.

Dr. Galloway, a surgeon, knelt opposite Dr. May, saying, "Trache?"

"Do it," May responded. "I'm not getting any response!"

Galloway pulled a penknife from his pants pocket and plunged it into the throat of the prone girl, sawing a crude hole in hopes of allowing her to breathe. He feared her airway was somehow obstructed, vainly hoping this might work. A little blood leaked out, but as he leaned close he felt no air flow from the hole. The lack of blood told him her heart had stopped pumping so there was no blood flow to spill out. Galloway looked up at Dr. May, softly whispering, "I got nothing."

"Goddamn it," May hissed, "what the fuck happened? Where's the paramedics, we need them now!"

Benjamin Weinstein, a radiologist, said, "They've been called. I sent Jonathon to the entrance to bring them as soon as they arrive."

Dr. Galloway stood up, even while May continued his chest compressions. He maneuvered to Dr. May and said, "Take a break. I'll give it a shot," gently pushing the exhausted May aside. May turned again to Taylor, anguish on his face. "What the hell happened?"

As Taylor spoke, he could see the crowd parting for the EMT crew rushing toward them. Finding his voice, Taylor shook his head, croaking, "I don't know. I, I ... I don't know. She was fine, and then she just fell. It seemed like she couldn't breathe. I tried to catch her, but I wasn't quick enough." Tears welled in his eyes. He asked, "Is she going to be okay? Please, tell me she will be okay!" Dr. May did not answer, rising and stepping back for the EMTs. He knew better, but now was not the time or place. He watched as they put Alisha on the rolling stretcher and rushed toward the waiting ambulance. He turned to Lucy, his wife, and said, "See you later." She watched him walk slowly in the wake of the emergency crew. She knew from his expression it was really bad.

Four

Dare was asleep when Jenna slipped into his room. Lost in the fog of sleep, he felt a very pleasurable sensation. He thought he was dreaming and did not want the dream to end. Slowly he swam toward consciousness, realizing this was no dream. His eyes focused on Jenna, naked and panting as she pleasured herself. Dare had known she would come over after the ball. It was her routine. He went with it, riding the wave to ecstasy. When she finished, they both were covered in sweat and breathing hard. They had no need to speak.

Dare's name was Darren Nakot. He was a tall man, standing six foot, three inches, with a head full of Black hair. Slender and dark by birth, he was an extraordinarily handsome man. His father was Dr. Kiaan "Kip" Nakot, a neurologist from the State of Goa in India. Dr. Kip was much loved and respected, teaching and practicing through Tulane Medical School. Darren (Dare to his friends) was bright and a good athlete. He excelled at soccer and swimming when young and still had the body of an athlete at thirty-one. But Dare was not interested in sports, leaving sports at an early age. He liked girls and preferred the guitar to physical exertion. He was a decent student, underachieving by all accounts. His test scores indicated keen intelligence like his father, but his teachers told Dr. Kip that he was content to get by, not stand out. He cruised through LSU, eschewing the rigors of Tulane academics.

After graduation, he used his father's connections to gain employment as a pharmaceutical salesman. He was smooth, polished, and so handsome girls tripped over themselves chasing him. His door was always open, and women came and went by the score. While Dare made good money, he had bigger plans. He was soon running a recreational drug business behind the cover of his pharmaceutical sales job. He cultivated friendships with doctors and nurses, hospital administrators, and New Orleans' society, learning who was gay and who was an addict. He supplied drugs, Blackmailed those susceptible, and leveraged those he felt he could manipulate. When he was twenty-five, he crossed paths with sixteen-year-old Jenna Dupreaux.

They met at a wedding reception in the Garden District. Jenna, blond and cute more than pretty, was flitting around and sipping champagne. In New Orleans alcohol is a part of everything, and no one thought anything of young Jenna sipping champagne. She spied the tall, handsome older man across the room and beelined her way over. She was entranced by the good looks of the man who stood chatting a few steps before her. She was not sure what she wanted and less sure of how to get his attention. She needn't have worried. Dare took one look at her and knew. He saw it in her eyes, a look he was accustomed to. From his perspective, he was looking at a teenage girl in a woman's body. Her age was inconsequential to him. She was buxom, cute, and clearly saw him as attractive. He extricated himself from his conversation and in one long stride was in her space. He asked her name and whether he could offer her more champagne. Jenna was all in, and soon they were engrossed in each other. As the evening wore on he asked if she would like to accompany him for a drink. This led to his car, his apartment, and his bedroom. He offered her a tab of Molly (MDMA, or Ecstasy) to go with her drink. She swallowed it down without a thought. The next thing she knew she was naked as he took her from behind. She was inexperienced, fresh, and enthusiastic. He rode her hard. The next day she reflected on the experience. He had used her, not gently. He had done things to her and she ... loved it. She wanted more. Over the next few years, there was much more, and she dug every second of it.

Five

Decker was sipping a cup of coffee from Petite Rouge. It was 7:45 on a Monday morning, and he was headed to the station. Bluetooth caller ID showed the ME's office, and he tapped the answer button on his steering wheel. Denise's voice filled the car: "Tox results in over the weekend. That Rex girl, she died of fentanyl poisoning. Not just a smidge either. This White girl had way more than it would have taken to kill her. No other drugs, teeny bit of alcohol. Like Doc Ray said, damn odd. You ..."

"Whoa, D, slow your roll. How much we talkin' here?" Decker said, cutting her off.

"About five milligrams, more'n two times the amount that would've been fatal. No wonder she collapsed. When that shit hit her, her respiratory system failed. She just stopped breathing."

"Does anyone else know this?" Decker inquired.

"Not yet. Doc Ray be here soon. He'll let the family know. No easy way to deliver that news. They likely to pitch a bitch. This is a heads-up, Decker. Yo phone gonna ring sure as my name's Denise Richards. It's just damn odd, is what it is."

"Thanks D, I gotta go. I'm at the station. If I get the call I'll swing by and talk to Doc. Y'all busy today?"

"Decker, we got more dead bodies than a dog got fleas. We ain't got space for all these stiffs. You best call ahead 'less you want to talk while Doc cuts."

"Roger that, D. I see enough shit everyday without visiting the butcher shop. I'll call."

"Be safe, White boy. You my next husband, ole Hank ever passes," Denise cackled. Decker punched end and stepped into the parking lot at the station. It was still early, a bit of chill in the air. Gulls swooped around looking for morsels dropped by cops getting out of their cars at shift's end. Good pickings in the mornings. Not much to do but eat donuts or beignets while cruising the streets at 4 a.m. Decker turned his mind to his cases as he strode inside.

Six

Declan O'Day was born in the Irish Channel in New Orleans. His father, Aidan, was a beat cop from the neighborhood. He died in an alley off Tchoupitoulis when Declan was seven, beaten to death. The case was never solved. His mother, Sophie, was just out of high school when she got pregnant with Declan. Her family was Irish too, living in the same area. She and Aidan were quickly married. Sophie was a pretty girl who was still a child when Declan was born. Her father was a drunk, a docks worker. A mean drunk, he lashed out verbally and physically at home. Sophie sought comfort away from home, and Aidan was her anchor. His death shattered her, and she began a long history of meaningless affairs. When Declan was twelve, he came home from school and discovered her having sex on the washing machine with their neighbor Bradan. Her feet were up in the air, Bradan with his pants around his ankles. The washing machine made a bump-bump-bump with every thrust. Declan grabbed the iron off a shelf and struck Bradan in the back of the head. Blood coursed down the man's back, and Sophie screamed as if she had been stabbed.

Declan was in a blind fury and continued striking Bradan with the iron. It was a relic, old and cast iron with no cord. Each blow did significant damage, and Declan continued the beating long past any movement from the fallen man. Sophie, naked and screaming, jumped on Declan's back in a futile attempt to stop the attack. Her shrieks were so loud someone called the cops. Soon Declan was whisked away in a police cruiser, and Sophie pleaded for her son not to be charged. Bradan spent time in the hospital for a concussion and several broken bones. He eventually pressed charges, and Declan was sent to Acadiana Youth Center for two years. He was in daily combat with the other toughs in the home. He fought off sexual predators and bullies, quick of temper and quicker with his hands. In time he was left alone, a solitary boy with no friends and no purpose in life.

When he got out he was hardened and angry. He suffered from depression, displaced anger, and a tendency to violence. Anything might set him off. Self-medicating followed; drugs and alcohol helping him to forget the bump-bump-bump that still rang in his ears. He never went home, preferring life on the street. He worked odd jobs for meal money, and the next two years were a haze. Aidan's brother, Gil, himself a cop, finally decided he had to do something. He had interceded for Declan several times, receiving calls from other cops who knew the story and did not want to see the troubled young man go to prison. The tipping point was Declan being caught in a drug haze in the Quarter, OxyContin in his pocket. Gil thanked the two beat cops and finally got Declan in his car. He drove straight home and spent the next two days with Declan tied to a cot in his spare room. When the drugs cleared Declan's system, Gil let him loose, and Declan spent the next week at Gil's pounding on a heavy bag that hung in the garage. Gil noticed the quickness and violence with which Declan attacked the bag. Declan had grabbed a pair of worn-out gloves off a shelf, and though he had no training, he made the bag jump. Gil had an idea.

That evening he drove Declan to his friend Cappy's place. Cappy was somewhere in his forties, a Black former boxer who now trained young fighters and worked with troubled youth at the Resolve Boxing Gym. Cappy had come from hard circumstances; he never knew his father, and his mother had six other children by different men. There was never enough money or food, and Cappy had worked from childhood on. His education was from the streets, and he knew what the young man, who now called himself Decker, was facing. Without a change in trajectory, Decker would be dead or in prison within a few years. He agreed to work with Decker as long as Decker stayed clean and off drugs. Over the next year, Decker worked relentlessly at Cappy's direction. He found it freed him from his troubled mind, providing an outlet for his anger and aggression. They talked daily, and eventually Decker opened up a bit. He told Cappy about walking in on his mother, Sophie, having sex on their washing machine. His anger, he said, stemmed from her seeking affection from outsiders rather than loving him. He felt she was focused so much on her grief that she did not notice how he was suffering too. They had no money for counseling, and it was never a consideration. Cappy's response surprised the young man. Cappy said, "Decker, life ain't fair. I know. I been on the street myself. My mama did the best she could, but we never had nothin'. Here's my advice: Get over it. Whatever it is, get over it. We cain't change our family or what's past. All we can do is work day by day to make our way. Studyin' on your past troubles don't do no good. So get over it, boy, or it will eat you from the inside out." As time passed, Decker came to see that Cappy was right. He still struggled with some depression and anger, but he knew putting it in the rearview mirror was his best course of action.

He was a natural boxer, strong and quick with a toughness bred in the Acadiana juvenile facility. Two years later he won New Orleans' light heavyweight title in a bout at the Superdome. He was left-handed, redheaded, and a mean motor scooter. He thought of Cappy as the father he never had, and with Cappy's guidance, he resurrected his life.

Seven

Decker learned of his father's death one morning in the second grade. It was recess, and he was playing dodge ball in the school yard. His teacher, Mrs. Warlick, called him in and sent him to the principal's office. She did not give him a reason, and Decker was afraid he had done something wrong. Mr. Jones, the principal, was waiting for Decker and led him to a chair. Jones was in his forties, a kind man who loved his job on most days. Not today, however, as he knew he was going to give young Decker the worst news imaginable. He did not know many details, only that Aidan O'Day was dead, beaten to death during his night shift for NOPD. Jones got a paper cup and filled it with water, handing it to Decker. He began, "Decker, you will be going home with your mother, Sophie, soon. She is on her way to pick you up. I'm afraid there's been an incident involving your father. She can tell you more."

Decker did not understand what Mr. Jones was telling him. He was not sure what incident meant, so he pressed, asking, "Mr. Jones, what's an incident? Did something happen to my Dad?"

"Yes, something happened. Your father is dead, Decker. I am so sorry to have to tell you." Decker flung the little cone cup and darted out of Jones's office. Tears streamed down his face as he ran blindly down the hallway. He was crying so hard he did not see Ricky Stepp, an older boy emerge from a classroom. They collided, with Decker falling to the floor.

"Hey, you little twerp, watch where you're going. I'll give you a fat lip, ya little shit."

Rage filled Decker for the first time. He had no conscious thoughts at the time, at least none that he could remember later. He stood up and hit Stepp as hard as he could, the punch catching Stepp in the stomach. It knocked the wind from the older boy, who doubled over. Decker started punching and continued until a teacher pulled him off the downed boy. By then Stepp's face was bruised and swollen, with one eye closing. Mr. Jones came running down the hall and picked Decker up; the boy was still trying to get loose and get to Stepp. Five minutes later Sophie O'Day picked Decker up and took him home. He did not go back to school for the next ten days. He did not know he was suspended for five days. He attended the funeral wearing a little white shirt and blue jeans with his Black school shoes. His hands were bruised, his knuckles raw. He never forgot the sound of taps played at the grave site. From that day forward the sound of taps made him angry and depressed. He had no idea why.

Eight

ecker had just gotten his po'boy sandwich and found a bench in the shade. He plopped down and was unwrapping it when two kids swaggered up and got in his space. Decker took a bite of his sandwich and sized the boys up. The closest one, a Black kid, was nearly stepping on his shoes, which annoyed him. He'd just given old Dub ten bucks that morning for a shoeshine, and he did not want this mook ruining his shine. He looked the kid right in the eyes, saying, "Kid, if you step on my shoes I'm gonna kick your ass. If you make me drop my sandwich … you do not want to go there." He took another bite.

The older of the two, a skinny White kid wearing a wifebeater T-shirt, sneered and said, "Trigga gonna kick yo ass less you give us twenty bucks. Ain't that right, Trigga?" Trigga was a good size kid, maybe five feet, eleven inches; big feet, wide shoulders, with the dead eyes of a street kid. He put on his best glare and said, "Yo, cough it up or take a beatin', cretin." Decker folded his sandwich back into its wrapper; now he was more annoyed. Christ, you couldn't even eat lunch in this city in peace. He was about to make a move when the old guy who ran the sandwich shop came out the door. He had a ball bat in hand, with dark smears on the business end. He said in a loud voice, "I told you two to beat it. I don't need you hurtin' my business. Git!"

The White boy sniggered, saying, "What you gon' do with that bat, old man?" His pal Trigga puffed up his chest, curling a finger: "Bring it on, old …" He never finished his sentence, as Decker kicked him in the nuts from a seated position. Wifebeater whirled to face the new threat, only to feel blows rain over his torso. Too many, too fast to count. He felt ribs break and was down before he got his fists balled up. Trigga writhed on the ground, unable to do anything other than moan. Decker walked away, picking up his sandwich without looking back. The old man walked over to the two street toughs, looking down at them and shaking his head. "You two got to be the dumbest sobs in town. You should be glad you only got what you got. That was Declan O'Day, light heavy champ here for three, four years in a row. If you'd made him drop his sandwich, you wouldn't be leaving here without the ambulance. God forbid you messed up his clothes. He mighta killed you. He's a cop, for cryin' out loud. The other cops call him DOA; that tell you anything? Stupid fucks. Get outta here and don't come back." He turned and went back into his sandwich shop, the bat dangling from his right hand. Ten minutes later Trigga was on his feet, still bent over as the two limped off down the avenue.

Decker got back to the station house hot, hungry, and frustrated. He did not like the idea that New Orleans was a place where you couldn't eat a sandwich on a bench without some bum bothering you. He flashed back to his years on the street as a juvenile. Had he done the same sort of shit? He tried to remember, but that only brought him down more. He had been wasted most of the time when he was not working. His memory was clouded, as had been his mind at the time. Booze and drugs had been his crutches as he tried to forget his father's death and his mother's promiscuity. He knew he'd been violent at times; he had the scars to prove it. His recollection was that for the most part he gave as good as he got, but there had been times when he was so messed up he could not defend himself and took a beating as a result. Surely he had not tried to strong arm folks like the two mugs he'd just encountered. He took a bite of the cold po'boy and realized he no longer had an appetite. He threw the rest in the wastebasket and headed for his car. Driving aimlessly helped, so he fired up the Scalded Dog. That's what he called his Mustang, the Scalded Dog. He left a line of rubber as he hit the streets.

Decker drove aimlessly through the city, no real destination in mind. Eventually he wound up at his Uncle Gil's house. He parked in the drive and let himself in with the key he had. He found Gil sitting in his recliner in front of the television. The channel was set to WWL, where Gil kept it virtually all the time. Gil looked up as Decker came in saying, "Man, it's good to see you, Decker. I sit here all day in front of this box watching the talking heads rattle on about everything under the sun. Biden's the new president; maybe things will change a bit, huh?"

Decker did not bother to correct him. He was used to Gil confusing dates and events. It was happening far more often these days. "How about some coffee, Gil?" Decker asked, walking into the kitchen. He found the Mr. Coffee was on and the smell of scorched coffee was strong. Gil had left the coffee maker on again, and the burnt residue of coffee was continuing to bake. Decker turned off the machine and washed the coffee pot. He made a fresh pot of coffee, fixing one for both of them. He made a mental note to check on supplies, as Gil rarely left the house anymore. It was hard to see the man who had done so much for him in mental decline. But there was no denying it. Gil had dementia, diagnosed by his physician and getting worse. Just another something to worry about. He was not sure what he would do with Gil eventually. There was no one else to look out for him, so the job was Decker's. They sat for a time, sipping coffee and not speaking. After an hour or so Decker left and locked the door behind him. The whole day had been depressing. He drove home and went out to jog away his troubles.

Nine

The next morning at 8:55, Decker's cell phone chirped. The display showed Bondurant, EH as the caller. Wondering how they had his cell number, Decker took the call, answering, "Detective O'Day ..."

A male voice responded, "Detective, E. Hunt Bondurant here. I'm calling about my daughter Alisha's murder. Her mother, Aline, and I want a full investigation. When can you meet with us?"

Decker was annoyed at the man's arrogance, although not the least bit surprised. He responded, "Mr. Bondurant, how did you get my cell number? More importantly, I don't know that there has been a murder. You're not in my chain of command, so I'm not free to meet with you unless I get orders to do so. No disrespect intended, but I have other cases and other priorities at the moment. I am sorry for your loss."

"Don't be impertinent with me, young man. I got your number straight from the mayor, whom I imagine got it from the chief of police. Of course there's been a murder. Our daughter did not do drugs." Decker heard what sounded like a struggle. The next voice he heard was a woman's, raw emotion making her voice crack. "For the love of God, Mr. O'Day, help us please. I'm sorry Hunt was so brusque. We're devastated. She was our world. We couldn't have other children, don't you see? She was special. Just a perfect baby, I still remember ..."

Decker cut in, knowing that she was about to build him a watch to tell him the time. "Mrs. Bondurant, I hear your pain. I deal with death every day. It's my job. But I can't just jump into the middle of a death in the family. My lieutenant would have my a—, my job. I'm not aware the death has even been classified as a homicide. I'd need directions from above to meet with you and to open an investigation. Surely you can see that, can't you?"

"Yes, yes, I understand there are channels. It's just so hard … her death at the happiest time of our life. I'll deal with Hunt and see if we can get you some authorization to talk with us. That's all I ask, as a mother. I'm sure you had a mother who cared, so perhaps you will understand the depths of my grief?"

Decker was silent for a long moment, prompting Mrs. Bondurant to ask, "Detective, are you still there? Hello?" All Decker could hear was bump-bump-bump. He pushed the painful noise in his head aside, saying, "Yes, I understand grief all too well. If I get the order, I'll meet with you. Again, I am sorry for your loss. Mrs. Bondurant, I have to go. Goodbye." He heard sniffling and an argument in the phone as the call abruptly terminated.

Ten

Twenty minutes later Lieutenant Leeks leaned out of his office, yelling across the room, "Decker, in here, now." Decker had a pretty good idea he was about to get the Carnival Queen case, as the press called it. He approached Leeks's open door, tapping as he entered. "Take a seat, Decker. I just got a call from Captain Crunch telling me to put someone on the Alisha Bondurant 'investigation' immediately, as in, priority status. He said her old man called you this morning and did not like your tone. The mayor called the captain, who told me to straighten your ass out and send you to see these folks this morning. He said, and I quote, 'Tell that mick pug to see the Bondurants ASAP.' Be nice, hear their story, and look into it a bit. The mayor reminded him that shit rolls downhill. Do I need to remind you that you are at the foot of the hill?"

Decker smiled at Leeks, shaking his head. "No, Lieutenant, I get it. Bondurant was just such an arrogant prick, like I was his hey boy, you know?"

"Sure, I know. All these rich fucks think the world revolves around them. He may not be far off, at least in this town. Daddy's head of Rex, got a container business that prints money, and is old New Orleans money. Mama is no different. Crunch knows the death is not yet classified as a homicide. Hell, for all I know the poor girl may have offed herself to escape Daddy. What I do know is you got to get over there, listen to their side of things, and see if there's anything to it. It may be a waste of time, but this is not a request. Crunch said, 'Now,' as in right fucking now. Got it? Everything else stands down until I give you the high sign."

"Roger that, Lieutenant. I'll call Bondurant and set up a meet. All's I know is according to Denise, Doc Ray says the death is odd. By the way, why do they call him Captain Crunch?"

Leeks grinned, wide, big yellow teeth flashing. "That one's easy. You ever meet Crunch, shake hands with him?"

"Naw, just saw him at my graduation ceremony, close as I've been."

"Well," Leeks continued, "you ever get close, look at his hands. They look like catcher's mitts. Big, industrial-size paws. Crunch was a beat cop back in the '70s. He and his partner rolled into Algiers on a call one night. Disturbance at Finn's Thirsty Pond, a real bucket of blood bar. Strictly White, mostly dockworkers. The kinda joint they gave you a knife at the door if you didn't bring one. Anyhow, Crunch and his wingman answer a call: fight in a bar. They step inside to an all-out brawl—blood, busted chairs, broken bottles all over the floor. Soon as they clear the door, the fight stops. This big, burly dude, closest one to them, says, 'No niggers allowed.' Crunch steps over to him, grabs his hand, and starts squeezing. The mook tries to squeeze back, but it ain't no good. Crunch is breaking bones in his hand; word is you could hear 'em popping. Mook goes to his knees, Crunch still squeezing. The guy starts bawling; Crunch don't even look down. He looks at the crowd and says, 'That'll be Officer Brimmer from now on. The rest of you cracker muthafuckas better not make a peep the rest of the night.' Crunch finally let go, and they walked back outside. The story got around. Ever since he's been Crunch, only now he's a captain. Now, go see the Bondurants before he comes over here and kicks my ass."

Eleven

Decker pulled into the driveway of the Bondurant house in the Garden District. It looked like a hotel to him. The style was Greek revival. It was two stories, stark white, with three huge White columns supporting the roof over the front porch. There were evenly spaced multi-panel windows, each larger than Decker, on the front facade. The side of the home featured a full-length porch, with the same massive white columns supporting it. The door was enormous; it looked to be old, made of oak, with a large brass knocker. The grounds were immaculate, with several monarch oaks, azaleas, and lots of flowers. Decker banged the knocker several times, and after a brief pause the door was opened by a man in full butler attire. He invited Decker inside, leading him along the hall to closed double doors. The butler knocked, and a man's voice called out, "Enter."

The butler swung the door open, and Decker stepped into the room. Oak paneling, leather-bound books, and oversized furniture. It reminded him of something from *Gone With the Wind.* A man in a blue blazer was standing behind a large table-type desk, and a woman rose to greet him from a chair off to the side. She rushed forward, clasped his hand, and said, "Thank you so much for coming, I'm Aline Bondurant," before Decker could utter a word. The man did not move, eyeing Decker with a measured gaze. Obviously this was E. Hunt Bondurant. He finally came around the desk and offered his hand. "Hunt Bondurant."

Decker shook his hand, saying softly, "Yes, I'm Decker O'Day. Pleased to meet you. Again, I am so sorry for your loss." Aline sniffled, dabbing a handkerchief at her eyes. He was afraid she would break down, but she summoned up a toughness Decker had not expected.

"Thank you. I must apologize for Hunt's imperious manner this morning. He forgets he's not running the world at times. We are in shock, barely functioning, don't you see?"

Hunt Bondurant remained aloof, saying nothing.

Decker shook his head, saying to Mrs. Bondurant, "No need for apologies, but thanks anyway. I know it's a terrible blow. Who wouldn't be in shock? Now, tell me the story." He sat in one of the leather chairs facing the desk. Aline settled beside him, and Hunt Bondurant took a seat behind the desk, saying, "Aline ..."

She pursed her lips as if thinking how to begin. "You know Alisha was our only child. I could not have more, much to our regret. A delightful little girl who grew into the most fantastic daughter anyone could ever have. She went to UVA ... the University of Virginia ..."

Decker broke in, setting the tone. "I graduated Tulane Law a few years back. I know UVA. Please continue."

The Bondurants exchanged a glance; Decker knew they got the message. He was not just a dumb grunt from the poor part of town. Aline continued, "She'd just graduated. Rex selected her as its Queen of Carnival. The King is Win Bentley. They got on famously. I was beginning to think they might become something more ... permanent. The Bentleys are one of the most prominent families in town. Win is just the nicest young man. He just got his MBA from Tulane. Everything was just splendid until that dreadful night."

Hunt broke in, anger in his voice. "No drugs. Ever! That's the thing that's killing me ... us. Alisha hardly took aspirin. I saw her tipsy once in high school. She was a fitness fanatic. She ran daily, swam, and played tennis. It just makes no sense."

Decker asked, "Is there any chance she was depressed? Down over something?"

Aline bristled. "Absolutely not. No, no, no. Ask Taylor Brinson, he was with her when it happened. He told us she was laughing, making light of the self-importance of certain people. That damn Jenna Dupreaux, most likely. She was as happy as she had ever been; she was a happy child from birth, never changed. No way did she kill herself." Decker could see red bloom in her cheeks, and she began crying softly. For his part, Hunt Bondurant sat stiffly, anger and frustration lining his face.

Before anyone else could speak, Decker responded, "I know it's difficult, but I have to ask. You want answers. I have none to give you."

Hunt spoke up. "Ask your damn questions. We'll have answers, or I'll have some heads on a pike. Aline and I know this will be difficult. It can't get any worse than it already is. We can't sleep, we argue. Christ, why not one of us? It's not supposed to be this way. Goddamn it, something happened. We don't know what or why. Now Alisha's dead."

Decker stood. He nodded as he got ready to leave. "That's enough for now. I'll see myself out. I'd like a list of Alisha's friends, the court, anyone who might know something. Can you email it to me? Here's my card." Hunt snatched the card, declaring in a loud voice, "It will be there by morning. Names, addresses, contact information. Whatever you need. Money is not an issue; if funds become an issue ..."

"No, that won't be a problem. I'll do my best. That's all I have to offer." Decker left the broken couple to their misery. He too was suffering emotionally. The bump-bump-bump played in his head the rest of the day. When he left work he went straight to the heavy bag at Resolve Gym. For a solid hour he attacked it with the violence of a man possessed. He exhausted himself to the point that he slumped to the floor, spent. Twenty minutes later, still drenched in sweat and soaking wet, he got in his car and headed home.

As soon as Decker was gone, the Bondurants tore into each other in their grief. Aline, crying and emotional, said, "You arrogant bastard. How can you live with yourself? We need him on our side, investigating. And what do you do? Talk down to him, act superior and aloof, which comes quite naturally to you."

Hunt countered, "Oh, for Christ's sake, Aline, I wanted him to understand that Alisha counted, that we are people of means and not the usual riffraff he investigates. You sit there begging and crying, neither of which does any good. At least I'm trying to get something done, to light a fire under someone's ass."

Aline stood and headed for the door, where she paused and turned. She said softly, "Yes, Hunt. I'll continue to cry and beg. I've lost the most important thing in my life. I hurt so deeply I wish I could die. So you light the fire and chap asses; I'll do the mourning for us both." She slammed the door behind her as she left.

Aline went to her car and drove to their house on Lake Pontchartrain. It was her special place, where she and Alisha windsurfed and roasted marshmallows on an open fire. It held so many summer memories for her. It was the one place where she still felt connected to Alisha, felt her spirit was there, that she would be there forever. She thought of Alisha stubbing a toe on the dock, crying out for her. Sadly, this was no stubbed toe. She spent the day on the dock, hidden behind sunglasses and a big hat. She watched the wind stir the lake, small whitecaps forming. Aline was not hungry, but she had a thirst that could not be quenched. She thirsted for knowledge. It was driving her mad: What had happened? Had Alisha hidden her drug use? No, she dismissed that out of hand. Alisha was into fitness, always active and working on her tennis or some form of exercise. Depression? Aline did not think so, although knowing the mind of another was next to impossible. She had sensed nothing but joy in Alisha

leading up to the ball. She had confided that she was beginning to find Win Bentley to be a deeper, more complete man
than the boy she had grown up with. That left two possibili-
ties for Aline to consider: The first was an accident, some
sort of unbelievable fluke which landed fentanyl in Alisha's
path. But how had it gotten into her system? It made no
sense. She would never have taken drugs, especially not in
the middle of the Rex Ball. Aline did not know much about
fentanyl; actually, she knew next to nothing. But she had
heard of drinks being spiked by the date-rape drug ... roofus,
puffy, no, roofie, that's what it was called. But fentanyl?
Could it be dropped in a drink or stuffed into food? How
fast did it act? Aline had a lot of questions and no answers.
She did have time, great gobs of it. It was all she had left. She
would use it to learn what she could about fentanyl and how
it might have invaded her precious Alisha. There had to be
an answer, if only she could find it.

Twelve

ecker had seen his mother, Sophie, sporadically over the years. She visited him from time to time while he was in Acadiana. She wore the same red dress every time she came to see him. He had no way to know that his mother's red dress was her tricking dress, the one she wore as she prostituted herself to supplement her income. Her visits were often separated by months. She came one Saturday a month into his sentence, the first time he saw her in the red dress. She had on bright red lipstick and smiled brightly as they led him into the visiting room. They hugged, and she gave him a candy bar, a Nutty Buddy, his favorite. She said, "Decker, my sweet boy, how are you? You look like you've lost some weight."

Decker did not want to tell her any version of the truth. He had lost weight, spending time in what was referred to as The Closet. You got one meal a day in The Closet if you were lucky. Some days you got nothing if the guards did not like your attitude. You were put in The Closet for fighting, stealing, and all sorts of misconduct. Decker was a regular in The Closet, which was a solitary room with a cot and a toilet. Cold water only in the sink and one blanket, an old wool thing bought from military surplus. It stank and had not been cleaned in years. Decker flashed on all of this and responded, saying, "I'm fine, Ma. This uniform is just too big, that's alls it is. How are you?"

Now it was Sophie's turn to lie. She replied, "Oh, I'm fine. I miss you a lot. I found a job cleaning rooms at the Dauphine Orleans Hotel. I don't make much, but I'm getting by. Decker, did you have a Black eye? Your eye looks yellowish, right in the corner. Have you been fighting again?"

"No, Ma. I promise. No fights." In fact, two weeks earlier two boys tried to rape Decker by pulling him into a broom closet. Both were older and larger, forcing him into the storage room. Decker broke free with one hand and grabbed a can of Lysol, spraying one boy in the eyes. The other punched Decker hard in the left eye, knocking him into some shelving at the back of the closet. Decker grabbed the first weapon he saw, an old ball-peen hammer, and went to work. He smashed the boy's kneecap with the hammer and struck the other one on the right shoulder, breaking his collarbone. He was in the process of doing a bit more body work with the hammer when the guards stormed in and overpowered him. He went to The Closet as a result of the fight. He actually did not mind it that much. He hated the majority of the other boys. Most were mean and stupid, on their way to becoming hardened criminals. The two who attacked Decker blamed him, and both spent a couple weeks in the infirmary following the fight. One had a shoulder brace to allow the collarbone to heal, and the other had his knee immobilized due to a shattered kneecap. Both had broken hands from blows with the hammer. Word was spreading that O'Day was not a kid to mess with.

Decker wanted to change the conversation, so he asked about his father's death. It was not the first time, but Sophie decided he needed to know the truth. She hoped it might help him stop fighting and get his life together. "Decker, there's no way to sugarcoat this. Your father, Aidan, died from being beaten in an alley off Tchoupitoulis Street. They never caught his killer. It was horrible, but he died doing his job. He loved being a cop and tried to do right by folks. He was a good man; I miss him deeply. I know all of this has been hard on you. I can't blame you. I just wish none of it happened. But it did, Decker. Now, I'm afraid you'll come out of this place a criminal. I know it's tough in here. I hear things, ya know? I'm sorry I let you down. I got my own struggles; I lost the house, your father ... now maybe you, too. I am so sorry." She started to cry, and Decker wept too. He was depressed and angry as they led him back to The Closet.

While Decker sat in The Closet, Sophie drove back to New Orleans. She was bitter, her life a mess. She hated her father and his stink. Dead fish and stale sweat still filled her nostrils, years after she had left home for good. She had few prospects; no education beyond high school, and she was no student, never had been. The only thing she had going for her were her looks. Maybe she could find a nice guy and still make it all work out. Yeah, maybe all was not yet lost. She decided a wee nip would lift her spirits. Plus, where else was she going to meet guys? The bar scene was all she knew. She headed for The Bent Elbow, a favorite haunt of cops and working men. She felt comfortable there, in her element. A tot or two and she'd be right as rain. At least, that's what her father always said right before he went on a bender.

Thirteen

The coroner's office was a tan building on the corner of Earhart Boulevard and South Claiborne Avenue, near Booker T. Washington High School. A cavernous place, 37,000 square feet with a pathology lab and office space aplenty. Decker pulled in to park at three minutes until two, when Doc Ray took his afternoon espresso break. He'd called ahead, set up the meet through Denise. Entering the building always gave him a shiver. It was kept cold for obvious reasons, and the smell was of death and chemicals. No amount of air freshener could mask the odor of the ruined bodies housed here. He walked into Doc Ray's office, tapping as he entered. Denise and Ray sat sipping espresso, silently savoring their brew. Denise perked right up. "Wanna cup?" she offered.

"Sure, why not? You guys buy the good stuff. What is that smell in here? Kinda funky sweet, with a tang ..."

Denise was rising from her chair, and as she reached for a Styrofoam cup she chirped, "I just came from the Happy Valley Yoni Steam. Slipped over at lunch. That smell ..."

Decker cut her off. "D, please. I just ate lunch. Forget that espresso."

Denise frowned, putting the cup down and stalking out the door, which she banged behind her. Doc Ray, ever placid, just looked at Decker and smiled. Decker shook his head, saying, "Jeez, she is a strong flavor. Sorry, bad choice of words."

Looking amused, Doc Ray retorted, "You really have no idea. It's all day, every day. What a piece of work that one is. Now, on the Bondurant girl. ... Time is flying, and I have lots more work left today. Here's what I can tell you for sure. She was a beautiful girl, twenty-two, and in top-flight physical condition. Good muscle tone, organs all looked fine. No brain issues and not drunk. She ingested a little over five milligrams of fentanyl. That stopped her breathing—just bang, she had no chance. A couple of doctors were right on hand, and they tried, but it was no use. The tox report showed a little alcohol in her stomach and system, but I would say it was de minimis. The fentanyl killed her. Of that there is certainty. The question is how did it get in her body? I have no answer to that. It's just damn odd."

Decker listened without interrupting. He really had no questions. He did not know what to ask, and there seemed little to be learned beyond what Doc Ray had said. He thought for a minute and queried Doc Ray with one last thing. "Doc, you been at this for a long time. What does your gut say? Foul play or some type accident."

Ray looked Decker straight in the eyes, saying, "It doesn't feel right. I can't rule this as a homicide, I've got no basis. But something's off. Healthy girl; Queen of Carnival, no traces of drugs in her hair or system. It does not fit. I'm leaving things open for now. I just don't know, but ... shit, it should not have happened. You hearing me?"

"Loud and clear, Doc. Thanks for your time. I'll go poke around in the society crowd, see what snakes I can find. There are always a few bad apples in any barrel. See ya around. Thanks again." Decker walked briskly out to his car, glad to be free of the smells that had assailed his nostrils.

In a pool hall named Sally's Balls, down near the Quarter, the Steiner brothers were doing a little meth. It was their kind of pick-me-up and made them feel powerful, in control. They were skinheads on the prowl for a mark. They needed cash, and Sally was their "no questions asked" fence. He was a mean son of a bitch, cheap and greedy. But he had cash and did not roll for the cops, qualities the Steiner brothers admired. Sten, the leader, said, "Hey, dude, see that?" He nodded toward an elderly Black woman pushing a shopping cart past the pool hall. She was moving slowly as she passed the front windows of the billiard room. They'd seen her before pushing that cart. She went to a little bodega and loaded it up before pushing it home.

Steen, the younger and dumber, said, "Yo, I see her. What?"

"You fucking moron, she has money. She only pushes that cart when she's headed to buy stuff at Pepe's place down the block. She has cash, dude, real green cash. Let's go get us some."

Sten led the way and Steen plodded dumbly behind. They caught her just as she came abreast of an alley and Sten punched her in the kidneys as hard as he could. She went down, and they were on her. Dragged her face down into the alley, grabbed her purse, and were gone twenty seconds later. They left the eighty-five-year-old woman lying in the filthy alley with scrapes to her face and bruised kidneys. They laughed all the way back to Sally's Balls. Maybe a little pool, score some good dope from Ice. Who knew what the night might bring?

Fourteen

In the days following the Rex Ball, Jenna put on her sad face at every opportunity. She avoided contact, appearing to grieve in private. She attended the funeral, wearing a Black dress, veil, and hat. She stood in front of the mirror for thirty minutes admiring her look before heading to the church. The whole thing excited her in a way she had never known. The killing, the acting, attending the funeral right in front of everyone. They knew nothing. It was sooooooo delicious. She knew she would visit Dare that evening. They had been enjoying a new level of sex; at least, she had. It was unbelievably good, leaving her sated but eager for another round. Dare had no complaints.

At some point it occurred to her that the actual murder had been as good as the sex that followed. She was smart; she knew that was abnormal, not the reaction she had expected before the deed. Beforehand, she had been all in with the idea for several reasons. She had desperately wanted to be the Queen of Carnival at the Rex Ball. Alisha, that bitch, had denied her the honor. She had hated Alisha for a long time, jealous of the girl's beauty and popularity. Jenna had plenty of male attention, no doubt about that. Yet in her mind Alisha always had the top spot. Alisha was very smart, besting Jenna academically. They were the two brightest girls in their pond in New Orleans, but she could not quite match Alisha's grades. They were valedictorian and salutatorian at Girls' Preparatory School, the private girls' school they attended.

Alisha went off to the University of Virginia, while Jenna had to settle for Louisiana State University. They both had fine college careers academically. They were in the right sorority, hung with a rich, mostly White crowd. They graduated on time and both returned to New Orleans. Alisha went to work for her father's company, while Jenna went to work for a local TV station. Jenna had aspirations to be a news anchor, adored by all of New Orleans. She would do that for a couple years, enjoy as many men as she could, and then settle down. She had her eye on Win Bentley, the King of Rex, that same year. Win was from a family with older roots than hers, going back to pre-Civil War New Orleans. The Bentley family was into everything: shipping, stevedoring, import/export, you name it. They had offices in ports across the country, including Los Angeles and San Francisco. Win was considered quite the catch among the female elite in New Orleans. He played tennis for Tulane, did well academically, and was a handsome fellow in his own right. Jenna thought that she could string him along for a couple years while she played the field, eventually marrying him and having kids. Not that she needed the money, but she would have anything and everything she wanted if she could make him hers. In the time leading up to the murder, Jenna sensed that Win was getting a tad too attached to Alisha. That was unacceptable. She would not come second to Alisha again. Jenna's rage had reached the boiling point. She had done what she needed to do. Like the sex with Dare the first time so long ago, when she reflected on the murder she ... loved it.

Fifteen

Gail Waites was everything White society disliked. She was a tall Black woman, with blunt features. Her weight moved between 180 and 200 pounds, far from the slim White females that dieted their way through life in New Orleans. She was bull strong, mannish muscles lurking beneath her skin. She had an enormous butt, and she drank like a fish. She drank to fight her own inadequacies, to escape the memories that haunted her from birth. Truth was, she was a functioning alcoholic. She struggled with her weight. She was gay, having a live-in Black lover. She was street tough, growing up in the Calliope Projects. Her life from birth was hardship, violence, and racial injustice. Her earliest memories were of a drunken man beating her mother and molesting her. Drugs, poverty, and prostitution were rampant in the Calliope. Yet Gail, flawed as she was, had made it out. She had dropped out of school in the tenth grade, eventually earning her GED and joining the NOPD as a street cop. From there she fought her way into a detective slot in sex crimes, working mostly in the projects. She got this gig only because no one else wanted it.

Now at thirty-nine, Gail slogged her way through the myriad sex crimes that occurred in the Black areas of New Orleans. Her live-in was named Jean Brown, a nurse at University Hospital. They had known each other since child-hood, growing up in a world filled with all the wrong things. Jean was three years her junior, and Gail had long been Jean's protector. Jean had a baby at sixteen, unmarried and with no support system. Jean had lived with several men over the years, all of whom beat her or took her money. Through it all, Gail had remained close to her, and a couple years back they became lovers and moved in together. Jean swore off men. They had done nothing for her other than inflict more misery. But Jean was a good mother from the beginning. As she scratched her way through school to a nursing degree, working two jobs, she had raised a beautiful baby girl, Anita. Gail had been part of that too, as they took turns with the baby and both had a hand in raising her.

Seven months before Alisha's death, Anita Brown was found dead on the side of Tulane Avenue early one morning. An autopsy revealed that she had sex sometime in the hours before her death. Rohypnol and cocaine were found in her system. The cause of death was an overdose of cocaine. Although listed as a homicide, no arrests had been made. There was no DNA in the vagina, although there were traces of lubricant from a condom. The body appeared to have been washed and re-dressed haphazardly. No one had seen anything, and there was really no evidence to follow. The case was just one more Black female dead of drugs on the streets of New Orleans. Jean Brown was suicidal for the first couple of months, but the hospital staff she worked with made sure she got the care and treatment she needed. She was now limping through life, hollow inside and bitter.

Jean Brown learned of the death when Gail returned to their apartment at 6:30 that morning. Jean knew Gail had been called out around 5:00 a.m. but had no idea why. As Gail came in Jean knew something was wrong. Gail was crying, her anguish apparent. Jean thought something bad had happened to Gail, but Gail pushed her down on the sofa, saying, "Jean, there's no way to make this easy. Anita is dead."

Jean thought she had misheard. It was not possible, not her Anita. Anita was doing so well, herself in nursing school and thriving. She shook her head no, screaming, "No, that's not possible. Anita is fine. I'll call, you'll see ..." frantically looking for her cell phone. Gail grabbed her by the shoulders and held her firmly. "Listen to me, Jean. That can't happen. I just came from University. Anita is dead. I got the call out and rolled up on a cruiser on Tulane Avenue. Anita was dead, honey, nothing anyone could do." She pulled Jean close, holding her as Jean wailed and thrashed about.

"Take me there, right now goddamn it. Take me down there now, you hear? I got to see my baby!" Jean was hysterical, but Gail knew she would not rest until she saw with her own eyes. She gently led Jean to her car and drove quickly to University Hospital, lights flashing, siren wailing. The scene was chaotic when they arrived, but Jean knew where to go and would not be denied. She pushed her way in to see Anita's lifeless body. She fell to the floor, weeping and screaming. Gail sat down, knowing the emotion had to play itself out. Several hours later, when Jean had calmed down, they were in the cafeteria drinking coffee at a corner table. Jean was wired, determined to tell Gail her feelings. Gail sat quietly listening as Jean rambled for over an hour. Much of her dialogue was to herself, Gail holding her hand with an occasional squeeze. Finally Jean reached the end of her mental journey. She seemed to quiet herself, and Gail thought she was done. After a couple minutes of silence, Jean focused on her like a laser, speaking quickly. "Gail, it's that goddamn Darren Nakot. Got to be!" Gail had no idea who or what she was talking about. Jean continued, "That muthafucka. That sorry muthafucka. He killed my baby. I know it sure as I'm sittin' here." She started to rise, and Gail jumped up and stopped her.

"Hold on Jean, just a damn second. You can't just run off and kill this dude," Gail said. "Who is Darren Nakot? Never heard the name."

Jean sat back down, gathered her thoughts, and continued. "Darren is a pharmaceutical salesman. Reps for the big drug outfits. His father is Dr. Kip Nakot, a neurologist. Dr. Kip is a prince, but that goddamn Darren. He's a snake, everybody says so. A real ladies' man, trail of panties you could follow for miles."

"Okay," Gail replied. "You don't like him, but sex is not a crime, Jean. Even if the man is hustling the ladies, that's a long way from killing Anita, you know? We just found her this morning. We don't even know the cause of death. You can't just run out and shoot this mutha. What makes you think he is involved?"

"Gail, I know my baby. We raised her ... you and me. She was a good girl. She knew better than to get in with some strange man. She was not a hood rat like we were, but she was street smart. She heard enough from you and me to know evil exists in this world. I had heard through the rumor mill here that Darren was hanging around, chattin' Anita up. I did not put much stock in it, really. He's White, rich, and got all the women he wants. Why he want to mess with my baby? She was just another Black girl to him."

"Yeah, so, that makes sense. I'm not seeing why you think he is somehow connected to Anita's death, hear?"

Jean replied, "I hear things, working here at University. I'm pretty much invisible to a lot of these folks. I mean, they know I'm around, but they talk like I'm not in the room. Just a Black nurse, who's she gonna tell? Nobody, is that answer. I don't know nobody, and they ain't worried I might say something to the wrong person. Hell, I don't know anybody would care, you feel me?"

Gail knew exactly what Jean was saying. They were alive, working alongside others. But they were nobodies; no one knew or cared who they might talk to at work or otherwise. "Go on."

"So I hear that Darren is bad news. Nobody really saying too much, but enough for me to put two and two together. Women, doctors, lots of folks in his orbit. Whispers about drugs, not the stuff he peddles during the day, you know?

Like maybe you want some weed, some blow ... call Darren. That kinda thing. Now the ladies are obvious. They practically steppin' out they panties when he walks by. But this other stuff. It makes me wonder. I got a bad feeling about that boy. He sniffin' around Anita, now she dead. Hear?"

Gail took Jean's hand and said, "All right, honey, I hear ya. Let me look into it. It's gonna have to be off the books. This is not my kinda case, at least not what I usually get handed. I'll see what I can find out. Meanwhile, don't do nothin' stupid. You kill that White boy, and they'll send you to death row for sure. That won't do anybody any good. Let me look. Trust me on this one. Let's find out the cause of death. Okay?"

Jean resigned herself to the facts. Her daughter was dead. Anita had been a good child. She made good grades, stayed out of trouble, and was well liked. She should have grown up, married, and had children of her own. Someone had taken that away from her and tossed her out like garbage. Killing Darren would not bring her back. Gail would look into it. She trusted Gail, had for a long time. Besides, she could always kill Darren Nakot later. She just needed to know for sure who had killed her baby.

Sixteen

ecker started his digging by meeting Taylor Brinson the following day. They met at Taylor's office, which was downtown. Taylor worked in the insurance business and could set his own schedule. He offered Decker something to drink, and they both settled on bottled water. Taylor walked Decker through his entire day leading up to the ball. He'd gotten up, gone for a jog, and met some friends for a sandwich at lunch. The afternoon was spent getting ready for the ball that evening. He picked up some dry-cleaning, got a haircut, and met at the starting point for the parade. The ride was nothing special, with the usual drinking and merriment. He took a shower before the ball, and he picked up his date, one of the ladies in the court. The ball opened as it always did, with the introductions of the King and Queen of Rex, with the court being presented as well. Decker stopped him there, asking, "Did you see Alisha early in the evening?"

"Yeah, I saw her. She was on top of the world. Looked fabulous, happy. Just normal Alisha," he replied.

"Any sign she was intoxicated or taking something?" Decker queried.

"No way. That was not Alisha's thing. She was never a drinker, and drugs are out of the question. I know the signs. Dilated pupils, slurred words, that kinda thing. Had a couple friends who got caught up over the years. She was none of those things. I still can't believe it. One minute she's laughing in my ear ..." Taylor choked up. Tears rolled down his cheeks. He could not speak for several minutes but finally continued. "She just dropped. I mean, dropped like a stone. I could tell she was not breathing right. Next thing I know I'm on my ass and there's a couple of doctors working on Alisha. I know Dr. May. The other guy ... didn't know him. They're pumping her chest, hard. Like there's no tomorrow. That's about all I remember. It's a fucking blur. That doctor poked a hole in her neck, then the paramedics grabbed her and were gone. Everybody was asking me questions and I ... I couldn't remember anything else. Nothing I could point to, you know?"

Decker ignored the question, posing this instead: "Who was around when it happened? Did you see anybody; or anything out of the ordinary?"

Taylor thought for a minute, responding, "No, I've tried a hundred times to remember something, anything new, different. Just nothing other than what I've told you. I'd had a few drinks, was happy, but not really drunk."

Decker watched Taylor closely as he changed tones, almost barking, "You had some drugs though, didn't you? Some fentanyl?"

Taylor didn't hesitate. "Fuck you. I hate drugs. Not that night or any night. I told you, I had some friends who got messed up in that shit. One fried his brain. The other died when we were fourteen; jumped off a bridge. So no, I didn't bring any drugs, and I didn't have anything to do with Alisha's death. Fuck you, man."

"All right, Taylor. I had to ask. Anybody in the court into drugs?"

Taylor's response was honest. "Probably a couple of them smoke weed; maybe a lot of them. Someone may do more, but if they do, it's not when I'm around. You can ask around. Maybe someone will spill something."

Decker stood, saying, "We're done for now. I believe you. But something may come back to you as time passes. That happens. Call me anytime if it does, okay?" handing Taylor his card. Taylor nodded a yes, and Decker left as he'd come in. He had nothing new, nothing he did not already know.

Seventeen

Gail and Jean grieved the death of Anita as any parents would. The pain was unbearable. There was no salve to be applied. They were, for the most part, alone with their grief. Anita had friends who attended the funeral and the gathering afterward at the church. They said the right things and promised to stay in touch, but no one believed they would. These kids had no real connection to the two older women. Neither Gail nor Jean had family support. They hadn't had any all their lives. They arose daily and went on with life because they were survivors. The autopsy and tox report showed Rohypnol and cocaine in Anita's system. Cause of death was a heart attack from too much coke. Anita had no residual traces of other drugs in her hair or system, and there were no signs of violence. She had simply ingested a lethal amount of coke, and it had killed her. The obvious question was how had that happened? How had she gotten to Tulane Avenue in the middle of the night?

Jean Brown still wanted to go after Darren Nakot, but Gail convinced her to let her do some investigating. Gail used any free time she had to work on Anita's case. The detective who was assigned to the actual case by NOPD was Billy Sims. Sims was a raw rookie, having made detective a couple months prior to Anita's death. Gail reached out to Sims, who agreed to meet her at French Truck Coffee on Chartres at 7:30 one morning. It was a block or so from the Royal Street Station, with a reputation for great coffee. Gail was there fifteen minutes early, and at 7:30 sharp a young man came in and walked directly to Gail, who was seated at a table. She had two coffees, one for him and hers, which she was halfway done with.

Billy Sims offered his hand, and Gail took it, pointing to the coffee and asking him to sit down. Gail judged Billy to be under thirty, fresh-faced and dressed nicely. Most of the male detectives were sharp dressers, Billy being no exception. Billy spoke first. "Thanks for the coffee, Gail. What's your connection to this case? I'm not too clear on that, you working sex crimes and all."

Anticipating the question, Gail produced a shot of Anita when she was two years old, saying, "I've known Anita from birth. Her mother and I grew up in the Calliope. I helped raise her. She's a daughter to me, Detective. This is personal."

"Fair enough, I get it. I'm happy to discuss it with you as long as you don't step on my investigation. Understood?"

"Clear as can be," Gail responded. "Not my intention. What can you tell me? Mind if I record this?"

"Yeah, I do mind. Take all the notes you want, but no recordings."

Gail picked up her cell phone, mashed a button, and pulled a small pad and pen from her purse. Seeing that, Sims began, "You got the tox report, right? Coke and roofie. No DNA, no fingerprints, lubricant in her vagina, most likely from a condom. No signs of violence, dumped on the side of the road. Near University, which best guess is the perp wanted her found. My thinking is she was alive when dumped, and the hope was someone would find her and get her into the ER. Didn't happen. You were at the scene, that's in the officer's report. My question is why were you there so early in the morning? Like you were the mother or something? Help me out here."

Gail did not blink, saying, "Her mother and I live together, not far from the hospital. The beat cop who found her knew I'm close with Jean, her mother. She called me. I went over, and then went to break the news to Jean."

Sims chewed on that for a minute before speaking. "Huh, live together as in roomies, or live together as in more than roomies?"

Gail frowned, but held her anger at bay. She replied, "We're a couple, not that it's any of your business. We don't hide it, by the way."

"Fine, just don't let the emotion lead you to interfere, that's all I'm saying." Gail nodded for him to continue.

"So far I don't have squat. No wits, no cameras on the dump site, lots of cars and trucks in and out that night. It's a hospital; folks come and go at all hours. She didn't seem to have any steady boyfriend, dated around a little best I can tell. Nothing serious. Word is she was a good student, nursing, well liked. No enemies that anyone knew about, and drugs do not seem to be a regular part of her life. Tell the truth, I kind of feel like I'm banging my head on a wall. What do you know?"

Gail considered the question. She knew he was likely to ask and had weighed what she should tell him. She knew he had talked to Jean Brown already and that Jean had pointed at Darren Nakot. He had held this back, and she was not surprised. Cops held their information close, especially young cops trying to make a name and climb the ladder. She had concluded that unless he told her, she would hold her silence on the matter. She would do her own investigation, his warning be damned. Gail shook her head negatively, saying, "I got nothing to offer. I'm clueless. Sorry I can't give you something to run with, Detective. Thanks for your time." The meet ended, and they both went on with their day. Gail never heard another word from Billy Sims.

Eighteen

Decker walked out of Taylor Brinson's office to a gray sky threatening rain. It was chilly that day, winter not having given way to the inevitable heat and humidity of New Orleans. Decker often thought the city's nickname should be the Big Greasy. When you were outside in the majority of the months in New Orleans, sweat, grit, and the smell of the river were unavoidable. He returned to his car, a restored '65 Mustang his uncle Gil had given him after his first title as light heavyweight champ of New Orleans. Gil had tinkered with the car for years, keeping it in a friend's barn outside the city. It was fire-engine red with a convertible white top. Gil was so proud that Decker had turned his life around he knew it was the perfect gift and the right thing to do. It was a young man's car. Decker, for his part, considered it his favorite possession, having grown up with little in the way of nice things. The Scalded Dog, that's what he called her.

He popped the trunk and retrieved his iPad. As promised, Hunt Bondurant had the information on all Alisha's friends and the court in Decker's email inbox the next morning. Decker figured he ought to make a run at the males in the court first. He pulled up Win Bentley's cell number and punched in the number. Bentley answered on the second ring, asking, "Who is this?" Decker identified himself and his mission, asking if he could meet with Bentley in the next day or so. To his surprise, Bentley invited him to head over. The Bentleys owned an office building on Lafayette Street in the Warehouse District. Decker prompted Siri to find the address in Google maps and headed over. Traffic was not too bad, and ten minutes later he pulled to the curb, finding a parking place within a block of his destination.

He strolled down the street hoping he would not have to walk back to his car in the rain. The receptionist, a smiling young woman with a pink strip in her hair, buzzed Win Bentley. Bentley came down a staircase and Decker met him at the foot of the stairs. Win Bentley was about five feet, nine inches tall, with brown hair in curly ringlets. He had a firm grip and appeared to be fit. Decker remembered that Aline Bondurant told him Bentley played tennis for Tulane. He looked as if he still played regularly. Win invited him upstairs, and they entered a conference room with a large conference table surrounded by leather chairs. Win offered water or coffee, choosing water for himself. Decker opted for coffee, needing a boost. They took seats, with Win saying, "Sorry if I sounded rude on the phone. I get all these sales calls. I thought you were one of those."

Decker nodded knowingly. "Those bastards selling extended warranties on cars are the worst. I intend to shoot the first live sales person I meet. Listen, thanks for talking with me. I need to hear your story for the day Alisha Bondurant died."

Decker saw the young man's shoulders slump, and his expression registered pain. Either he was a damn fine actor, or he was genuinely pained by the memory. Win launched in, "Christ, I hardly know where to begin. Alisha and I grew up together; known her since kindergarten. We never dated until the court thing this year. I ..." His voice trailed off, and he began sobbing, burying his face in his hands. It was a full three minutes before he regained control and wiped his eyes with a linen handkerchief. "I'm sorry. It's still so fucking raw. I liked Alisha. Hell, I might have been falling in love. She had a beautiful spirit. She was gorgeous, for sure. But there was a lot more to her than looks, I can tell you that. She made everybody feel better about themselves."

Decker broke in. "Win, I don't mean to be rude. But I do need facts. I need to know everything you did that day. Where you went, people you saw, the parade, the ball, all of it."

"Yeah, sure, I get it. Am I a suspect?" he queried.

Decker nodded, saying, "Everyone is a suspect until we can rule them out. You, the court, every damn person there."

"Fine. I have nothing to hide. I need to know what happened too. I don't think it will change anything, but we all need to know." For the next hour and a half Win Bentley told Decker everything he could remember about his day. He had not been in close proximity when Alisha collapsed, so he had no insight there. He did not use drugs but admitted to smoking the occasional joint in college. He did not do so often because of his tennis. It cut his wind, and he needed every advantage he could get to deal with bigger, more powerful players. He described the aftermath and the solemn mood that drowned the evening's fun. He had gone to the hospital with most of the court. He thought the only members who did not go with them were Lee Jordan, Greg Bingham, Jenna Dupreaux, and Ross Wilbanks. Lee Jordan had fainted, and she was herself taken to the hospital as a precaution. Greg Bingham was a doctor and had left the ball right after the ambulance. Ross Wilbanks and Jenna Dupreaux had left early too, Jenna telling everyone she had a migraine come on when she learned Alisha had collapsed. No one seemed to know any details, and when they learned Alisha had died, they all went home.

When Win finished his story, Decker inquired, "Win, was any member of the court into drugs? Don't bullshit me, Win. You do, and I find out you lied, I'll come back and kick your ass."

Win had no idea Decker was a boxer, but he could see fierceness in Decker's eyes. The intensity of the man's gaze made the hair on his neck stand up. He thought

Decker looked a bit like Sean Penn, except bigger and more muscular. Decker had a large, craggy nose that had obviously been broken and fiery red hair. Scar tissue ran along both eyebrows. Win weighed his options for a moment. He could lie or fudge the truth and hope that his money and status insulated him from violence. In the end he decided to come clean for two reasons. Alisha was one. The second was that he realized they both lived in the city. Sooner or later Decker would catch him alone, and that thought won the day. He nodded, saying, "Yeah, a couple of folks will tune up from time to time. I know Susan McCormack is fond of X. She likes to hit the raves, dance all night. Crawford Stilton does a bit of blow, though I don't think he uses regularly. Mark Konrad is a bit of a stoner, big into weed. Those are the ones that come to mind. I'm sure all the kids have experimented a bit. Hell, I know they have. We all had money and went to a million parties through the years. But I think everyone is pretty clean. I don't recall seeing anyone using that night, and fentanyl is really outside our zone. I could see someone buying something laced with that shit and not knowing it. But I can't see our crowd really using it. Just not cool in the circles we run in, you know?"

Decker nodded, handing Win a card. "Call anytime if you hear or remember something. No matter how small, inconsequential; whatever. If it seems odd, I want to know. I hope you've been straight on the drug angle. You seem like a decent kid, but I will fuck you up if you're lying to me."

Win was quick to respond, "Yes sir, I understand. I'll call if anything comes up." Decker said nothing else, finding his own way out.

Nineteen

Gail was ten when her first act of violence occurred. She had been coming up the outdoor stairwell at the Calliope, where she lived. On the fifth floor the old man grabbed her, dragging her into shadow in the corner of the stairwell. Gail knew what was coming. The all too familiar stench of body odor and alcohol jammed her nostrils. She tried to pull free, but as had been the case many times before, the old man was too strong. His rotten breath disgusted her, and she felt his fingers rammed into her vagina. She knew it would not last long, so she relaxed and went away mentally to her safe place. True to form, the old man was quick. He always rubbed the offending fingers under her nose when he was finished, adding insult to injury. He cackled a bit, and pushed Gail down roughly in the corner. But this time was different. He did not wobble back down the hall to his apartment. He turned to the stairs and headed down.

Gail was on her feet in an instant. She caught him on his third step, down. Her chest level with his mid-back, she slammed into him as hard as she could, arms extended. He flew forward headfirst, striking his head on the stairs below and pinwheeling down to the next landing. Gail stood for a moment, breathing hard and looking for him to rise and come after her. She was ready to run, but there was no need. He lay motionless in a heap, arms and legs akimbo. Gail turned and rushed up the steps to her apartment, where she let herself in. She found the cheap whiskey under the kitchen sink. She poured a full glass, gulped it down, and sat down to do her homework. She did not think further on the incident. She knew she would have to deal with him later. He would be angry and might hurt her worse. But that would be then; this was now and that was her life.

A few days later Gail heard some of the older kids saying old man Rice had died from a fall on the steps. She edged closer, wanting desperately to hear more. There was not much more to be heard. The kids said everyone assumed he had fallen and banged his head. Everyone knew he was a drunk, mean and cranky. His death was little more than another dead body in the B. W. Cooper Housing Development, colloquially known as the Calliope. Gail felt nothing upon learning of the old man's death. She was glad she would not have to endure his torment any longer. For the rest of her life, she despised bad breath and BO. She was not fond of old men, either.

Later that year Gail's mother died of a drug overdose. She was twenty-six years old, dead from a hot shot of heroin. They found her on a bench in Calliope, the needle still sticking in her arm. Years later Gail thought of the funeral service. Maybe ten people there, most of whom she did not know. No flowers on the altar, and the minister seemed to be in a rush. Gail was with her aunt Leda, with whom she was living at the time. They did not go to the gravesite. Leda later told Gail her mother was buried in the pauper's cemetery. She did not know the gravesite, only that it was somewhere outside New Orleans. Leda had no car, and Gail never visited the grave as a child. It was only after she was grown and had her own car that she made the drive to Potter's Field. She finally found the little white cross with her mother's name. She put a rose on the grave, said a short prayer, and left without seeing anyone. Like her mother, Gail was anonymous in sea of poor people who were trampled daily.

Twenty

Jenna Dupreaux's first act of violence was much different than Gail's. She was at the Presbyterian Church, where all the right people attended. She had no trouble accepting the idea that she was one of a special group of people; she was sure of it. She was eleven years old and had a crush on John Grey. John was her classmate in Sunday school, and for the past few Sundays Jenna had been trying to get his attention. John acknowledged Jenna politely but seemed more interested in Sally Davies. That Sunday she did everything she could to attract his attention before they went to the basement where their Sunday school class met. John followed Sally around like a puppy that morning, totally ignoring Jenna. Jenna experienced her first fit of rage, although she was too young to see it as such. She just knew her flirtations were being ignored, and she was getting angrier by the minute. She tried getting between John and Sally, and John rebuked her saying, "Jenna, move. Quit being a pest. Go bug someone else." Jenna felt the color rise in her cheeks as her face flushed red with anger. Enough was enough.

When the teacher called for them to come downstairs to the class, Jenna made sure she was right on John's heels. As they descended she took a quick step down, making sure she bumped John firmly from behind. John lost his balance and fell forward, breaking his arm and knocking one front tooth out. Several other kids fell when he fell into them. Fortunately, they only skinned knees and hands.

Alisha Bondurant saw the whole thing unfold right before her eyes. She was sure Jenna had caused the accident on purpose and angrily confronted her at the foot of the steps. Jenna burst into tears, denying the accusation. The Sunday school teacher was panicked, fearing that John was badly hurt. She shushed the girls and sent Alisha off to alert parents and to bring help. Alisha hustled off and shortly returned with John's parents in tow. They rushed down the stairs to their son, who was now holding his arm and crying as he sat on the bottom step. Alisha would not let it go, continuing to insist that Jenna had done it on purpose. Jenna turned on the tears again and steadfastly denied that it was anything other than an accident. John's parents scooped him up and took him to the emergency room. He had his arm set. Several days later he had oral surgery to replace the lost front tooth.

Jenna's parents immediately took her side, dismissing Alisha as a little girl with a big imagination. They agreed to cover the expenses of John's treatment, insisting that it was only the right thing to do in the face of such a terrible accident. From Jenna's perspective, she learned several things. The first was that she had to be more careful in the future if she intended to harm someone. The second was that her natural response of crying was a great cover and made her a sympathetic figure, even though she was guilty as sin. But the third thing she learned surprised her: She had acted to hurt another person ... and she liked it.

That night Jenna's parents lay in bed discussing the day and what to make of it. Jenna was fast asleep; she usually fell asleep within a minute or so of climbing in bed. Nothing troubled her, that was for sure. Jenna's father, Patrick, turned to Suzanne, his wife, and said, "Do you think it's possible Jenna did push that boy down the stairs?"

"Certainly not, Patrick. How could you think such a thing of our Jenna?"

Patrick pushed his glasses down off the bridge of his nose so that they rode just above his nostrils. He spoke carefully. "Well, she has been going on a lot about him lately. How much she likes him, and how he does not seem to know she exists? I mean ... do you think it was maybe a little aggression, like ... she bumped him so he would notice? Maybe too hard, and he fell?"

Suzanne bristled. "How can you say such a thing? Jenna is the perfect child. She gets everything she wants. We love her, dote on her even. She has looks, brains; she has it all. She's sweet as sugar. It's just not possible it was anything other than an accident."

"Suzanne, she has a temper. Remember that time in the baby pool where she held that baby's head underwater? You had to jump in and pull her off him. He was coughing up water for several minutes. He ...."

"Damn you, Patrick. That was years ago, and she was just a baby herself. She was five. She didn't know what she was doing. Besides, he kept splashing water and it was messing up Jenna's hair. She got mad, that's all. Just a kid thing. Don't you ever mention that to me again. I want the best for Jenna. She'll have the best schooling, the best clothes, the best everything. I intend to mold her for success. She'll have a grand life. But we have to protect her. That's our job, do you hear? I don't care about this Grey boy and his tooth. It's an accident, that's all there is to it. We'll pay his expenses, and it will blow over. In a couple years no one will remember, unless you make a punching bag of our daughter. I won't stand for it. You get that through your thick skull. I will not allow you to injure our daughter and her reputation in any way. Damn you to hell."

With that Suzanne flung back the covers and stomped off downstairs. For his part, Patrick did not know what to think. He wanted the best for Jenna. He knew Suzanne was a bit of a narcissist and prone to fits if she did not have her way. He hoped Jenna was not cut from the same cloth. He turned out the light on his bed stand, but sleep did not come easily. He was worried and had no real idea what to do.

Twenty-one

Decker followed up his meeting with Win Bentley by calling Crawford Stilton. He got voicemail and left a message asking Stilton to call him back. He then called Mark Konrad, who answered the phone after four or five rings. Konrad sounded very stoned. He had difficulty understanding who was calling him but finally agreed to see Decker. He lived with his parents in a bungalow behind the main house and told Decker to comer over around 4:00 p.m. Decker pulled into the Konrads' driveway and followed it down the side of the house. He stopped when he saw the bungalow and walked over. Mark Konrad answered the door in boxer shorts and a Mötley Crüe T-shirt. The odor of weed was overpowering, and Konrad was obviously stoned. He invited Decker in and rambled his way through the day of the ball, to the extent he could remember it. He was nowhere near Alisha when she collapsed, saying he was likely out behind the building smoking a jay.

It was hard for Decker to get much from Konrad, but everything suggested that Konrad was a harmless stoner who was too lazy and inept to do much of anything. He readily admitted smoking a ton of weed. He did not work and had no desire to. His main focus in life appeared to be staying stoned and listening to music. Several times he used an app on his phone to turn the volume up to deafening even as the interview progressed. Finally Decker snatched the phone and threatened to smash it to bits if Konrad did not provide him answers. That worked, and he got more information in the next ten minutes than in the preceding thirty. Konrad stated that he did not do harder drugs like blow or smack, and fentanyl was not something he had experience with. He did agree that Crawford Stilton was the one among the court that he had seen do a line of coke from time to time. Eventually Decker gave up and left. He did not believe Konrad had the ambition to do much of anything and lacked any reason to harm Alisha. He left and drove straight home to change clothes. The weed had thoroughly invaded his pants and shirt, and he showered and changed, glad to be free of the smell. He tossed his clothing out on his patio to air out.

He talked to a couple more members of the court without much success. Ross Wilbanks confirmed taking the Dupreaux girl home with a migraine. He said he dropped her and went home to bed himself. Bingham, the doctor, described getting to the hospital and being told that Alisha was dead on arrival. He told Decker that he had been talking to Mr. Bondurant when the incident occurred. At least, that was the best he could tell, trying to reconstruct a timeline. The problem was that no one was really looking at the time during the ball, and everything was in flux as it is in every Mardi Gras ball. How could you pinpoint a drop of rain in a rainstorm? Decker felt like he was spinning his wheels, wasting time.

Twenty-Two

ecker called Crawford Stilton for two days and got no response. Stilton was avoiding him. Not unusual as many folks did not want to speak to the police. Still, he was the only person that others pointed to as doing coke, which was more in the league with fentanyl. He figured Stilton would at least have a possible source who supplied his drugs. That was worth a look. He emailed Taylor Brinson, who promised to ask around about locating Stilton. Three hours later Brinson texted him saying Stilton was known to frequent a bar in the Quarter named The Green Parrot, known to locals as The Parrot. He was familiar with The Parrot and knew drugs were rumored to be available from some of the regulars. He ate dinner at a taco truck close to the station and headed over there about 7:00 that evening. He had nothing else going and thought it was worth a look.

He entered The Parrot and took a seat at the bar. He ordered beer from the tap, and handed the barmaid a ten dollar bill. He asked, "You know a guy named Crawford Stilton, comes in here regular?" She snatched the ten and spoke without looking in that direction. "That's him over against the wall, in the suit." Decker took a sip of his beer and eased around to look that direction. He saw a well-dressed guy in a suit seated with a stocky White guy in sandals, jean shorts, and a T-shirt. T-shirt had long hair, a Fu Manchu mustache, and a gold chain around his neck. Decker made him for a likely dealer. He had that look. Picking up his mug, he walked directly over to their table.

"Gentlemen, invite me to sit down," he said, relaxed and easy. He set his beer on the table top. Fu Manchu knocked it to the floor, breaking the mug and sloshing beer on Decker's shoes and pants.

"Get the fuck outta here. This is a business meeting," growled Fu Manchu. Suit tried to stand, but Decker pushed him back down in his chair. Decker shifted his eyes back to Fu Manchu, who was reaching for his pocket. Decker moved like a cat pouncing, hand flashing as he grabbed Fu Manchu by the hair and smashed his face into the table top twice. Suit heard the man's nose break and blood poured from his ruined nose.

Decker took one step back, saying, "You get blood on my clothes and I'll break both your hands. Now shut the fuck up unless I ask you a question. Miss, bring a bar towel over please. This gentleman has developed a nose bleed." The barmaid did as instructed, bringing a soiled bar towel over and throwing it toward the bleeding man. He caught it and pressed it against his nose, trying to stanch the bleeding. Decker pulled a chair from another table and sat down a couple feet away. "Let's start over. I'm Detective O'Day. Mr. Stilton, I've called you for two days and have nothing to show for it. Why is that? You avoiding me?"

Suit shook his head vigorously no, whining, "I've been busy. Too busy to call, man. I'm sorry, my bad."

Decker smiled saying, "Really, A full forty-eight hours goes by, and you can't make a cell call to see what I want? That's a load of horseshit. Your buddies tipped you I'd be calling, and you been on the down-low ever since. Now you got me thinking you had something to do with Alisha Bondurant's death. Maybe we need to go talk down at the station."

"Whoa ... no, man, no. You got this all wrong. I had nothing to do with that chick's death. I swear to God I didn't. She had nothing to do with me, didn't really like me, you know?"

"Yeah, I can see that. I don't like you much myself, and we just met. But word is you're into blow. Blow's not far from fentanyl, so maybe somehow there was a mix-up, and Alisha winds up dead. Maybe you meant for it to happen."

"No way. No fucking way. Okay, I admit it. I do a toot of blow time to time. Fentanyl's not my thing. Swear it man, you gotta believe me. I had nothing against that girl. If you talked to the others, you know I was not within fifty feet of her when it happened. Me 'n' Lizzie, Elizabeth Woods, were dancing near the band. Check it out, Lizzie'll tell ya."

"Don't worry, I will. Is this fine-looking gent your supplier? He's got the look?"

Fu Manchu growled through the towel. "Don't say a fucking word, or I'll ..." He never finished as Decker half rose and pivoted off his left foot, his right fist hooking into the towel over the broken nose. It knocked Fu Manchu over backward to the floor.

Decker looked down whispering softly, "Shhhh, I did not ask you a question. Now, Crawford, is this piece of excrement your supplier?"

Stilton looked like a cornered animal. He was clearly worried about the guy on the floor and consequences. But the look in Decker's eyes frightened him more. There was something ... predatory in those eyes. They were the eyes of one of the raptors in the bird house at the New Orleans zoo. The meat eaters; the ones with long talons and fierce eyes. In the end he gave it up. He named the fallen man, whom he called Ice, as his supplier. He swore he only bought coke, and Ice confirmed that when he regained his senses. Decker, not interested in a petty drug bust, left the two shitbirds in The Parrot where they belonged.

Twenty-three

Decker spent the rest of the week running down the other male members of the court. He had little to show for his effort as the week ended. He went to the gym early Saturday morning and sparred with a pal for three rounds. He then did fifteen minutes on the heavy bag and finished with a lift. He always did the weight work last. It tended to tighten his muscles, which he then stretched out over the next few minutes. He planned on grabbing a steam later in the day. He headed out for a late breakfast. He drove over to the Waffle House on Canal Street, ordering eggs, toast, and Black coffee. Fueled up, he headed home and napped for the next hour. He ventured out to the library and a music shop, bringing home several books on New Orleans history and a classical CD. His uncle Gil had introduced him to classical music. He liked it immediately, with the soaring notes and lovely melodies. Now his uncle Gil was suffering from dementia. Gil, who had been instrumental in saving Decker from himself, was struggling to live independently. He wandered around the neighborhood aimlessly. Decker found his bathing habits spotty, and the sink often was piled with dirty dishes. He flashed back to the charred coffee in the pot on his last visit. The CD was great until a mournful song began to play, filling Decker with anger and dismay at life's unfairness. He switched it off and went to bed, where he lay for an hour or two before finally falling asleep.

Sunday morning broke to a bluebird day. He carried coffee onto the balcony and enjoyed the sunshine. He retrieved his iPad and began planning his next moves in the investigation into Alisha's death. He composed an email to the Bondurants and sent that. He figured he would bum around a bit longer and head over to the station to write up his weekly report. Double L, his supervisor, would want to see what he had been up to. Decker knew Captain Crunch was up Leeks's butt, pressing for any information to keep the mayor off his back. It was 10:25 in the morning when he got the call: shooting at Chabad-Lubavitch, a synagogue on Freret Street. It was a May Day call, and Decker grabbed his duty bag and headed for his car. There were blue lights everywhere when he arrived. Multiple ambulances, people screaming and crying. Utter chaos. The mass shooting at the Chabad Temple sucked the air from the city for months to come.

Twenty-four

Decker could get no closer than two blocks away in his car. He whipped to the curb and leapt from his car. He left his plug-in flashers gyrating; they joined an already crowded horizon of red, yellow, and blue lights. He walked briskly toward the temple, gun in hand, hanging loosely at his side. He was unsure if it was still an active shooter scene. It was beyond anything he had encountered in his time with NOPD. He saw horror on the faces of cops and EMTs as he got closer to the temple. He had his badge on a lanyard around his neck for all to see. No one stopped him, so he pushed past paramedics and EMTs rushing bodies to waiting ambulances. He finally spotted a senior officer he knew from the precinct closest to the temple. He beelined over to Sheila Wallace, a lieutenant who was speaking rapidly into a handheld radio. He heard the words "At least twenty dead. ... No, I have no fucking idea how many more! Send more buses, goddamn it. It's a bloodbath. No, no ... the shooters are gone. I don't care whose balls you have to break, get more men and ambulances here now. I gotta go. Yeah, will do."

"Lieutenant, what the fuck happened?"

She turned at his voice, and he saw a steady stream of tears rolling down her face. "Fuck it all, goddamn it. Two perps hit the temple with ARs. It's as bad as I saw in Afghanistan. The motherfuckers killed kids, women ... the rabbi. I think the only thing that stopped them was they must have run out of bullets. This was not a fucking message—they wanted to kill every Jew in the place. They goddamn near succeeded. I gotta go. I don't have command. That'll be Captain Winston. He's around somewhere. See if you can make yourself useful.

I ... I ... fuck, I gotta go." With that she walked off toward a crowd of cop cars, leaving Decker unsure of what to do next. He knew that in these situations someone had to be in charge or it made things more chaotic. He sprinted toward the temple, holstering his weapon. Up the steps, stepping in blood; no way to avoid it. There were so many blood trails he lost count. Inside, an abattoir waited.

He spotted Captain Winston and hustled over. Winston knew him from his boxing, being a huge fight fan. Winston saw him, did not hesitate. "Decker, get out front. Take charge, I'm putting you in the lead out there. Tell anybody that questions you I will put my foot up their ass. Put the word out. No fucking media. Kick some ass if you have to. I've called the chief. This is gonna be national. FBI's coming; we need to move fast before they bigfoot us. Get going. We'll talk later." Decker barreled back outside and started barking orders. No one questioned him. They were in shock, moving numbly like robots. As the day wore on, the horror of the shooting became clearer. He saw so many body bags it seemed they would never stop coming. He heard someone say the rabbi had been killed, along with a cantor and several elders. Worst were the kids. He could not tell ages from distance, but he could see some smaller bodies being carried out. His sense of horror turned white hot with anger. This was killing for its own sake. Not sport, not war; just brutal taking of life randomly based on proximity to the shooters. He could not wrap his mind around someone shooting worshipers in a service on a bright blue Sunday morning. He had several confrontations with media trying to slip in to get a better story. Decker had to use restraint as the cameramen and reporters refused to take no for an answer. He finally got enough cops to hold them back as morning turned to afternoon. Multiple helicopters filled the sky and the sun baked down causing tempers to flare. He thought the day might never end.

Twenty-five

Decker stayed at the scene for the next ten hours. The flow of bodies carried from the temple was nonstop for the first hour or so. Eventually he saw crying children being escorted from the side of the building in a herd. Mothers and cops alike were crying, and the children looked blank. Decker knew most, if not all, were in shock. It was as grim a scene as could be imagined. The cops wrestled distraught parents and people rushing to the scene. The media had the story and was feeding like sharks on a whale carcass. Decker made sure none of them got inside the temple for pictures, but he knew with so many cell phones the carnage would be on the news within hours. He had no idea of the body count and was suffering from dehydration when he finally made it home.

He grabbed two bottles of cold water, drinking one in a long gulp. He dropped his clothes on the way to the shower. He scrubbed so hard he felt like he was peeling skin off. Then he stood under water as hot as he could tolerate until the tank ran out and the water turned cold. Still he stood, now shivering like he had a fever. It occurred to him that he might be in shock, so he stepped from the shower and toweled off. He got his iPad and googled how to treat shock. He took a couple of muscle relaxers and got in bed. He propped his feet up on a pillow and got under the covers. He told Alexa to turn on the classical music and to turn off the lights. At length he fell into a troubled sleep, dreaming of monsters chasing children down dark passages.

At 5:00 the following morning Decker awoke to his cell phone's haptic notification announcing a message had been received. It came from somewhere outside his bedroom. He sat up, wiping at his eyes. They were matted, and he rinsed his face in the bathroom before finding his cell phone on the table in the kitchen. He had a voicemail from Double L telling him he had been put on special assignment under Captain Winston. He was to report to the Tulane University Police Department at 2650 Ben Weiner Drive for a briefing at 7:30. Wide awake, he made coffee and turned on the news. He turned to WWL Channel 4, the CBS affiliate. The anchors were all over the shooting, with crews still on site and a helicopter overhead. They did not have accurate numbers on the dead and wounded, but they had cell phone video of the carnage inside the temple. It was gruesome, and Decker rushed to the bathroom, throwing up his coffee. He heard the anchor say, "Sources close to the investigation report over thirty dead, many more wounded. A press conference is set for 9 a.m. at police headquarters on Broad Street. We will have more details as they are available." Decker returned and turned off the TV. He was already wired and it was only 5:30 in the morning.

He changed into shorts, T-shirt, and running shoes, pulling on a headlamp which he wore on a band around his forehead. Out the door into the still dark streets of New Orleans he plunged. He always ran with a fanny pack with a pistol and his cell phone tucked inside. He did not expect trouble, and he ran for an hour in solitude. In his mind, he could hear the chaos and the screams from yesterday, with the occasional intrusion of bump-bump-bump. He ran harder and finished back at his house, breathing hard. He showered, dressed, and headed for the Waffle House. He knew he needed to eat. It was going to be a long day.

Finishing breakfast, he drove straight to the Tulane Police Department. He knew where it was located from his days at Tulane Law. Arriving at 7:20 he found a beehive of cops. He learned that a command center had been established there due to the proximity to Chabad Temple. Large coffee urns were in plain view, with the ubiquitous donuts and pastries atop folding tables. Cops were milling and munching. He took Black coffee and found a seat in the large room where the briefing was to be held. Eventually an old cop named Radford ambled over and sat down beside him. Sergeant Radford was in his sixties, of medium size and with a bulbous nose suggesting he was fond of a pint. He asked, "Decker, how's Gil doing? I heard he's having some memory problems."

Decker nodded saying, "Yeah, Sarge, it's not good. I'm not sure how much longer he can stay in that house by himself. He doesn't eat right; his hygiene is lacking. I have to remind him to take showers. I'm afraid he'll fall in the shower and kill himself. His balance is fucked up; he's too damn stubborn to use a walker. It's a mess."

"I know," Radford replied. "Christ, my mother is near ninety. You think she uses a walker? Hell no, says she will when she 'gets old.' I keep asking her when that might be, and she just adds two years to her age. Been going on for at least ten years now. Anyways, you still boxing?"

"Yeah, sorta. I work out and spar at Resolve Gym. I try to get there four, maybe five times a week. No fights or anything. This job keeps me too busy to train for that kind of thing. But I keep fit. Beating on the heavy bag helps me relieve stress, keep my mind clear. All the crap we see daily, you know?"

"Damn right I know. I drink; only way to wash all the shit outta my head. Lots of old cops eat their gun. I ain't gonna do that, unless they stop making Jim Beam. If that happens, I'm in the crapper for sure. Maybe I can get by, see Gil one day soon. Tell him I asked, ya hear?"

"Will do, Sarge. It'll make him smile if I catch him on the right day. See you around."

Twenty-six

Winston walked to the podium at 7:30 sharp. He was trailed by several men Decker did not recognize. They wore suits, white shirts, and ties. He knew the FBI was on the scene. Winston called the room to order and began speaking: "Yesterday at approximately 10:05 two men with blue medical masks and ball caps approached Chabad-Lubavitch Temple with assault weapons. They shot two men who were outside as lookouts dead as soon as they exited their vehicle. They ran inside and killed an old man right inside the front door. From the position of the body, we believe he was trying to get to the panic button on the wall closest to the doors. It would have locked the whole place down. They entered in a two man stack. We got that from several witnesses. One immediately sprinted down the aisle and killed the rabbi and several others close to him. He then turned to his left and began systematically shooting: women, children, whoever. We know he fired a full thirty-round clip because we found an empty near the front row. The second man turned to his right and started shooting at the back row moving forward. As of now, we have forty-six dead with seven more circling the drain. There are many more wounded who will lose limbs, be in chairs, the whole fucking nine yards. Fortunately most of the younger kids were not in temple, having been taken to other rooms for age-appropriate teaching. I want to introduce Special Agent Bill Kearney out of New York. He specializes in domestic terrorism and will now brief you on what he and his team have learned so far. Give him your full attention and cooperation. Word from on high is that anyone sandbagging is gone. No excuses, no second chances. Agent Kearney, the floor is yours."

"Thank you, Captain. I am Bill Kearney, and I have a team on the ground. We got here last night, and most of my guys and the techs are still on site. Here is what we know so far. The shooters had training, likely military. They did this with a military precision that we do not see in most domestic attacks. They were both capable marksmen. They hit what they shot at without wasted fire. That made this attack especially deadly. The tactics they used, one started up front to his left and the other started at the back to his right. A classic pincers move: nowhere to run, maximum damage, and they were not shooting in the direction to shoot one another. They were there to inflict as much death as they could within a three-minute window. The whole thing, start to finish, was four minutes tops, maybe less. They used two thirty-round clips each inside the temple we think. We are still working to determine trajectories, lines of fire, that sort of thing. We are recovering spent brass and looking to recover bullet fragments and anything else we can find. The caliber was .223, same as the M16 used by the military in Vietnam and around the world. But these guys did not do the usual spray and pray. We are almost positive each shot was single fire, with a target in sight. Bear in mind that as this unfolded people ran and crawled, trying to hide. It was complete bedlam, yet these individuals retained composure and shot at acquired targets time and time again. That suggests to us special forces type training, men who had seen combat up close and personal somewhere. The brass is not helpful so far. It appears to be common .223 ammunition that is available in most every state and abroad."

Kearney paused, saying, "Questions so far?"

One of the cops asked, "How do you know the window of the shooting so precisely?"

Kearney responded, "The first shot was heard at 10:05. We have an old lady who works at the temple and was in her office when she heard the first shot. She grabbed her cell phone and noted the time as she called 911. She heard intense gunfire over the next several minutes and then it ended abruptly shortly after 10:08. She had crawled under her desk, fearing a sweep of the building by gunmen. Every other person we have talked to puts the timing about right."

A detective Decker knew asked, "What was their mode of transportation? Did they drive, walk, bicycle ...?"

"We believe they were dropped off somewhere close by a white van. We are looking for cameras that surround the area and will know more as we get the footage analyzed. How they escaped is another question; we have no answer to that one yet. We're trying to determine if they left via a different entrance than the one which they entered through. It's possible they simply walked away. Or had a car parked somewhere they could get to pretty quickly. NOPD had officers on scene in less than 5 minutes, which is darn good for early on a Sunday morning. By then these guys were in the wind. Obviously the criminologists will be on site for an extended period, likely days. We know from experience that time is critical, but these things can't be rushed. It's often the smallest thing that puts us in the hunt. These guys were pros, no question in my mind. It goes without saying they are armed and dangerous. They may have acted alone or as part of a larger group. Your commanders will give you assignments. I caution you: Keep your head on a swivel as you work this case. If you stumble into something, back away and call. If it's a group, they'll have watchers around to give sit-reps. If you get close they will kill you if they can. This op was as professionally done as I have seen, here or in my time in the military. Be careful out there."

Captain Winston stepped back to the podium, issuing some orders and designations. He finished by asking for

Decker O'Day to see him after the meeting at the front. The meeting ended with cops huddling and talking, some heading for the exits and others still sitting unable to move. Decker stood and moved forward toward Captain Winston.

Twenty-seven

Decker approached Captain Winston, who was engaged with Bill Kearney. Winston noted Decker, and as he finished his discussion with Kearney he motioned Decker to join them. Winston said, "Let's step into this office," pointing to a door to their left. They filed in, and Winston pulled the door behind them. He said, "Coffee? I need some." They all got coffee, and Winston motioned for them to sit down. Kearney shook Decker's hand and reintroduced himself. Once seated, Winston continued, "Decker, the chief tells me you've been assigned to the Carnival Queen investigation. Bill, that's a local debutante who died in the middle of a Mardi Gras ball. Drug overdose killed her. Decker was Tulane Law and knows some of the society folks. He's been knocking on doors. Decker, Bill and I want you to work this Chabad case as you do that. Bill will explain."

"Please do, I'm confused," Decker responded.

Kearney looked at Decker as he spoke. "Decker, I know this may be a surprise, but hear me out. I do this all over the US, wherever we have a domestic attack by terrorists, homegrown. We study these people, and we have developed a lot of knowledge and understanding in doing so. It is common to almost all terrorist groups to have a hierarchy. There are leaders, and there are foot soldiers. Just like foreign terror, someone has to be the brains of the operation. For this case, we are working it in layers. I've got the NOPD using some of their undercover to hit the bars and strip joints, that type thing. We've got a kid who can pass for a college student working the student angle. There are multiple levels to this investigation. You don't need to be concerned about all that.

Your place is using the cover of the Carnival Queen to probe the society folks. Ideology is always at the heart of terrorism. Something motivates these folks in a powerful way, and they come to believe that violence will help their cause. Lots of psychology involved, but you get the idea. We want to work the money folks and society to see if anybody in that crowd is funding or assisting. We think you can do this in the context of your investigation and they won't see you coming. If we just start knocking on doors and asking rich folks if any of them are involved, word will get around and they'll go radio silent. Just shut it down, sit quiet, and wait for us to leave town and NOPD to move on. You see my point?"

Decker nodded, saying that he did. He certainly knew that the elites closed ranks and talked among themselves. He did not know much about ideology and terrorism, but it made sense. He agreed to do his part surreptitiously, and for the next hour he listened while Kearney tutored him on the finer points and how to inquire without appearing to be doing so as a cop. Kearney finished with a reminder: "Decker, if you get too close and these folks feel threatened you will be in danger. It may come from someone on the street, at your home, or anywhere else. Folks tied to this mass murder have made it clear that life is inconsequential to them. They won't hesitate to take you off the board if they feel threatened. You hear me?"

"That goes without saying. If they'll kill a bunch of folks in a religious service who are minding their business, one Irish mick won't trouble them. I'll be careful. Who do I report to?"

Kearney wrote his cell number on a card and handed it to Decker, saying, "Call me anytime. Keep Captain Winston in the loop as you go. Good luck, son." They all filed out, and Decker went on his way.

Twenty-eight

icky Elrod and J.R. Pine were stoked. They had carried out their mission and gotten away clean. They spent Sunday night in their rooms at the casino in Biloxi with escorts, lying low. Now they were sitting in the Crystal Pistol. The Pistol was a strip joint with relaxed standards and friendly girls. Drugs were available through the right connections, and the beer was flowing. Back in Black blared from the speakers as a lithe young girl shimmied up and down the pole in the middle of the stage. They had a pocket full of cash and rooms at Motel 6. It was going to be a long, fun night. J.R. was from Arkansas, Blue Eye to be exact. He was a White supremacist from birth, his father hating Blacks and other Brown types. He'd grown up hunting and was a crack shot when he joined the service at eighteen. He was tougher than a hickory nut, eventually joining the special forces and serving several tours in the 'Stan. He and Elrod, who went by El, met and bonded during training. El was from somewhere in Florida, one of those small redneck trailer parks. El was not into the White supremacy like J. R.; he just liked killing folks. That was his motivation for joining the service in the first place. Where else could you get training to kill, get to actually engage and kill and get paid for it? He could not spell ideology and could not have cared less.

Tonight they were throwing back beers and shots. They figured to get laid; several girls had already suggested as much. Something about the danger, it seemed to burn the panties right off girls of this type. They knew better than to drive drunk and could walk to the motel from the Pistol. Knowing no one could hear themselves think with the music so loud,

El leaned over and yelled in J.R.'s ear, "Goddamn, that was a kick. I still got wood from yesterday. Hoo-fuckin- ah!"

J.R. was the brighter of the two and likely not quite as fucked up as El. He turned quickly and pulled El close, yelling, "Shut the fuck up, El. You wanna spend the rest of your life in stir? Drink your beer and keep your mouth shut. You know the fuckin' rules; mission security is job one. How many times I gotta tell you that?"

Elrod grinned, knowing J.R. was right. He nodded and threw back a shot. He reached out and snagged Glitter, pulling her roughly onto his lap. Glitter did not object, picking up a fiver lying on the table and stuffing it in her garter. She giggled, saying, "Buy me some champagne, handsome! I'm damn thirsty." El was all in and hailed the server, who soon returned with a short bottle of the cheapest champagne that could be had. El forked over fifty bucks and squeezed Glitter a bit harder. "Gonna do you right, girlie. Brace up good, ole El's bringing it tonight." Glitter rubbed his member, took a swig of champagne, and said, "Big talk. That's what all you boys are. Anyways, you can have whatever you want, long as the cash keeps flowing."

"Fair enough. Where's my beer?" The party continued until the Pistol closed at 4:00, after which the men and their companions wobbled over to the Motel 6 where the fun continued.

Twenty-nine

It had been two weeks since Alisha's death. Jenna was coming down a bit, the high having faded as time passed. She realized she was not Queen of Carnival and never would be. That was a disappointment. On the plus side of things, Alisha was gone, good riddance. Win Bentley was in a bad place; Jenna saw opportunity. She would be the white hat, helping Win in a time of turmoil. She was not ready to marry him, but she could kill two birds with one stone. Sex was always good with Jenna. She reveled in her femininity. Win was a nice-looking man, and she was sure she could seduce him. She was very adept at finding weakness, like all psychopaths. It was as if the gods whispered in her ear telling her the weakness she needed to exploit. His was obvious: sadness and loss. She had the cure and knew how to use it.

It was the Wednesday following the shooting at Temple Chabad. Jenna phoned Win at the office and asked if he wanted to have a drink after work. Win was a bit surprised. He had known Jenna for years, all the way back to preschool with Mrs. Betty. She had never shown much interest in him, even though they ran in the same circles.

Jenna had always been Jenna, focused on herself. He hesitated before agreeing to meet her at a wine bar near his office. The Pressed Grape was a yuppie wine bar and at 6:00 that evening he sat down at an outside table where Jenna was already sipping a Pinot. He ordered and Jenna took the lead, telling him how sad she had been since Alisa's death. It surprised Win a bit, and he thought maybe Jenna had more depth than he had realized. For Jenna, she felt she was putting up good cover and sneaking through Win's defenses as well. She poured out her trauma over the death. Soon she and Win were crying, and she grasped his hand, giving it a squeeze as he opened up on how it had affected him. The evening rolled by, and they drank more wine. When Jenna felt the time was right, she asked Win if he would drive her home, claiming to be tipsy. Win agreed, and when he walked her to the door, she turned into him and kissed him full on the lips. He responded, and one thing led to another. Soon they were in Jenna's bedroom, and Jenna treated Win to the wildest sex he had ever experienced. Jenna congratulated herself on a job well done. Win fell fast asleep and Jenna played a life of privilege and travel in her mind as she drifted off.

Thirty

ecker left the briefing at Tulane PD and walked to a bench outside. He sat down and scrolled through his contacts, finding the number of his Constitutional Law professor at Tulane. He punched call, and to his surprise, Ali Kesten answered on the third ring. She obviously had caller ID, answering, "Decker, hello. Good to hear from you. What prompted this call? I figured you'd be running at Mach speed with the terrible event at the temple?"

"As usual, you're spot-on, Professor. I just finished a briefing at Tulane PD. We're using it as a command center on the temple shooting. I was wondering what you know about terrorists and their motivations ... their ideologies? I need a better understanding if I'm to do my job correctly."

Kesten did not hesitate. "Absolutely, I'll be glad to share a bit of what I've learned on that subject. I have a ten o'clock class. Can you come by my office at eleven thirty? I'll bend your ear over coffee."

"Thanks, professor. See you at eleven thirty." Decker had time on his hands and walked to the Howard-Tilton Library. He inquired at the front desk about books and terrorism. He was directed to a section on that subject and thumbed a few books until he found one to his liking, *American Zealots*, by Arie Perliger. He started reading and was soon lost in concepts he knew little about. Eleven o'clock rolled around quickly, and he met Ali Kesten in the hall outside her office.

Professor Kesten smiled at Decker as they shook hands. "Good to see you, Decker. Coffee?" Decker nodded, and Kesten moved to her Keurig and popped in a pod. "Gevalia, excellent coffee. Now, on to the topic of domestic terrorism.

I know you're busy, so I won't waste your time. Most domestic terrorists are motivated by their beliefs. It can be White supremacy, religious extremism, anti-government views, you name it. Whatever their beliefs, they use those beliefs as a foundation to justify their violence. It is very likely anti-Semitism is behind the attack on Temple Chabad-Lubavitch. That is obvious to even the most uneducated. One point that you need to keep in mind: those who carry out the attacks, the soldiers if you will, are not necessarily totally into the ideology behind the attacks. For example, take the January 6 mob. Many of them have later said they got caught up on the rhetoric, sort of a heat-of-passion defense. Does that make any sense?"

"A great deal of sense. You're telling me the shooters may or may not be zealots. But almost to a certainty those who provoked them and organized the attack are total anti-Semites, right?" Decker asked.

"Precisely. You were always quick. The leaders will likely hate Jews with a passion. Understand, they may hate other groups as well. It is common among extremists to hate multiple perceived enemies. I would guess that the head of the snake is White, likely fairly intelligent, and may even be educated. There may be others involved who base their hate on personal experiences or perceived slights. But with an attack like this one, on a temple and with the obvious goal of mass deaths, you are very likely looking for neo-Nazis or Nazi sympathizers."

"Huh," Decker intoned. "I didn't know there were many Nazi sympathizers still around."

"Oh, yes," Kesten continued, "there are lots more than you realize. Does the name Father Coughlin mean anything to you?"

"No, who is he?"

"He's dead. He was a Catholic priest and radio announcer way back in the '30s. He was a fascist, anti-Semite and believed that Jewish bankers ran things. He was immensely popular at one time. It was estimated he had an audience of 30 million followers, many working-class folks and blue-collar Catholics. His message reverberated with them. He eventually got in trouble with the Catholic Church as his leanings grew more radical. But he was a powerful figure and reached many with his notions of anti-Semitism." Decker was taken aback.

"Is that true, you're sure?" Decker inquired.

"Every word. You can check it out over at the library. Also, many members of Congress were Nazi sympathizers. Burton K. Wheeler from Montana being one of the most powerful. A guy named Rogge was heavily involved in finding and prosecuting Nazi war criminals. He identified twenty-four American congressmen, Wheeler among them, who had strong ties to the Nazis. The Nazis were doing what the Russians and Chinese are doing today. Lining the pockets of political heavyweights who then champion their cause. Truman ultimately had Rogge fired from the DOJ on the belief that the American people could not handle the perfidy and betrayal of so many prominent politicians. This stuff is not new. It was here when we were born, will be here when we're gone."

"Well, I'll be damned. That's news to me. American Nazis, I had no idea. Any other revelations I need to know about? My part in all this is talking to rich folks. What else do I need to know?" Decker asked.

"Excellent question. There's always a money angle. Whether it is to fund the actual attacks or spread the lies and propaganda. Someone is putting up some bucks, or they are getting money from somewhere. One last thing. Be aware that the anti-Semites live in all walks of life: businessmen, clergy, academics, you may find them anywhere. Keep an open mind as you go."

"Thanks a ton, Professor. I have a totally new perspective. This was time well spent. I'll go now and let you have lunch. Take care."

Kesten replied, "I will. You do the same. These types are extremely dangerous." Decker pulled the door shut behind him, shaking his head in amazement at what he had just learned.

Thirty-one

On the Friday following the temple massacre, the investigation got its first tiny lead. A girl of fifteen, who had been interviewed earlier, suddenly remembered that she had seen the letters EL on the boot of one of the shooters. She had been toward the front of the temple when the shooting started, taking cover under a bench on the opposite side of the aisle from where the shooter up front had been firing. He was shooting in the opposite direction, and she realized that when she heard "Go, go, go" from somewhere toward the back, the shooter paused. She could only see his boots and when "Go, go, go" echoed through the temple, the shooter turned to face the back of the temple. He paused only for a moment before sprinting toward the rear. In that brief moment, she saw the letters EL written in what she thought was black Magic Marker. They were plainly visible against the tan color of the boot's upper. Then he was gone, running down the center aisle. No more firing occurred, and the girl remained frozen until officers found her later cowering under the bench. Her interviewer had told her at the end of their session that things might come back in bits and pieces due to the trauma of the actual shooting. She awoke Friday morning, startled as this tidbit that emerged in her sleep. She called her interviewer, and by 9:00 a.m. Bill Kearney had this piece of information. He did not know what it meant, but it was something, thank God. The girl was unable to say for sure if the letters were lowercase or capitalized, but she was sure of the EL. And for the rest of her life the letters EL standing alone would cause her to shake uncontrollably.

Decker decided that based on his new orders, he would focus on the parents of the court rather than the members. It had to be done, and since no one was sure if there was foul play involved, the order did not matter so much. He also knew it highly unlikely that any of the court were involved in funding the attack, especially given how busy they would have been in the months leading up to Mardi Gras. He decided to call Crawford Stilton's parents first and was able to reach the mother at home. She agreed that he could drop by around 4:30 that afternoon. She would call and make sure her husband came home a bit early. Punctual as always, Decker knocked on the front door of Mr. and Mrs. Roe B. Stilton at precisely 4:30. He was greeted by another butler. He was beginning to get the idea; these people had lots of money. He followed the man to a sunroom on the back of the house. Mr. and Mrs. Stilton rose to greet him. "I'm Roe Stilton. This is my wife, Nancy."

Decker introduced himself and told them he had been tasked with looking into the death of Alisha Bondurant.

Roe Stilton continued standing, saying, "All very well, but why talk with us? We are not involved in any way. Neither is Crawford. Do we need an attorney?" Clearly the word was out among the elites. Decker sensed the wagons circling, the wariness of Stilton.

"I don't know if you need an attorney, Mr. Stilton. I'm assigned to ask questions and knock on doors. If you're not involved, you shouldn't need an attorney."

Stilton countered, "Crawford called. He was shaken up by your rough behavior. We will not tolerate being bullied about, do you understand me?"

"My hearing is quite good. You might ask Crawford about his choice of drinking buddies, by the way. Now, are you going to answer my questions, or shall we go downtown and have this discussion?"

"Is that a threat?' Stilton asked, puffing up a bit.

"It is not. Mr. Stilton, I don't threaten people. I do my job and keep my head down. Now, how about it?"

Mrs. Stilton joined in, "Oh, for heaven's sake, Roe, let the man ask his questions. You're just prolonging this. Sit down!" Stilton sat down, but looked as though he had a steel rod stuffed up his rectum.

"Are you aware that Alisha Bondurant died of fentanyl poisoning?" Decker asked.

"What? What are you saying?" Mrs. Stilton was clearly shocked. "Fentanyl? Isn't that what they give cancer patients for pain? Was Alisha ill?

"No, quite to the contrary, Mrs. Stilton. That is why the whole thing is so odd. The autopsy showed she was perfectly healthy, yet she died of a massive overdose of fentanyl."

"We know nothing of that," Roe Stilton said. "The very idea. It's offensive that you're here, insinuating our involvement."

Decker was getting weary of the little man's puffery. He replied, "Let's cut to the chase, shall we? I know Crawford was busted for cocaine last year. I know something is sealed in his juvie file. I know I found him in The Parrot last week with a scuzzy drug dealer named Ice. So stop all the horse-shit smoke and mirrors stuff. I'm not interested in your son unless he has some connection to Alisha's death. Do you understand me, Mr. Stilton?" Decker could see the color drain from Roe Stilton's face. Tears formed in Mrs. Stilton's eyes.

Silence prevailed for a minute, then Roe Stilton spoke. "Yes, all right. Crawford has had some issues. Christ, we've tried so hard. Gave the boy everything he ever wanted. But he had nothing to do with Alisha. He swore it. He said Alisha didn't like him. He was nowhere close to her when it happened, you can check."

"I already did. But the drug angle is the only thing we have to follow at the moment. I'm not accusing Crawford or you. I recognize that the city is tense right now, with her death and the temple massacre." Decker was looking directly into Roe Stilton's eyes when he mentioned the temple shooting, looking for a response. Something flashed in Stilton's eyes; quicker than a hiccup it was gone.

Nancy Stilton jumped in. "Horrible. Simply horrible. How do people do that sort of thing? We're all on edge. But Crawford is a good boy. Really, he is. Roe and I have given him all the best. He's just young, Detective. He'll grow out of this stage, I know he will."

Roe Stilton found his voice. "Of course he will. He's a Stilton, after all. Good stock, goes back a long ways here in New Orleans. I'm afraid that will have to do for today, Detective. Nancy and I are upset enough, what with the mass murder and the Bondurant girl. If you have more questions, we'll contact our lawyer and speak to you in his office. Am I clear?"

Decker smiled in a way that made the Stiltons recoil ever so slightly. Something predatory in the smile, back of the brain, lizard instinct that flashed, "Danger, danger, danger." Rising, Decker said quietly, "Clear as crystal, Mr. Stilton. Thank you for your time. Good evening."

Thirty-two

In the weeks following Anita Brown's death, Gail Waites did everything she could to find answers. She had Jean Brown making subtle inquires around University Hospital. Jean had her ears open and tried to pick up gossip, but the going was difficult. They both had full-time jobs. Gail was all over the place chasing down perverts and rapists. She felt as if the worst of humanity floated in the sewer in which she swam daily. Alcohol and Jean Brown sustained her. She had nothing else, and she knew she never would. She and Jean faced many of the same hurdles: Black women of limited means with no access to most of what New Orleans had to offer. No great meals at fancy restaurants. No lunches with girl friends at the Club, or fancy houses in the Garden District. None of the finer things in life were available to her.

Over the course of several months, they were able to gather a few bits of information. Darren Nakot had been seen talking to Anita on several occasions. But no one had ever seen them outside University Hospital. No one had seen them doing anything other than talking. Talking was a part of what Darren did in his sales job, so that was a nonstarter. Jean did learn that a multitude of females in the hospital had succumbed to Darren's charm, this group being dubbed The Harem by the rumor mill within University. Despite her best efforts, Jean could find no one who put Anita in The Harem. Many did not care for Darren, seeing him as a manipulator. Yet envy at his looks and success could very well explain this dislike. No one accused him of any crimes and in many quarters he was quite popular.

Gail was able to learn one morsel that she overheard on a foray into the narcotics division. She was trying to get a lead on a child molester and was talking to Dre Cole, a narc. She and Dre were in the coffee room getting coffee when two narcotics detectives wandered by. She heard the name Nakot and quickly hustled to the hall and stuck her head out. She caught the tail end of a conversation as they disappeared into an office. "Fucker is too smart to be caught. Slicker than owl shit, is what he is." The door closed, and Gail turned back to see Dre close behind. "What was all that about?" he asked.

Gail trusted Dre, saying, "You know Jean's daughter died and was dumped on Tulane Avenue?"

"Yeah, I remember something about that. So?"

"I heard the name Nakot as those guys went by. Caught the tail end, before they closed the door. One of them saying, 'He's too smart to be caught, slick as bird shit,' " Gail answered. "Right when it happened, Jean blamed Darren Nakot, a pharmaceutical sales rep. Didn't really have no basis, just a mother's gut instinct. We been tryin' to get answers, but you know the system. Walls go up, and we got no authority. I'm off the books on this one. I'd really appreciate if you keep your ear to the ground on this Nakot dude."

"No problem," Dre replied. "I'll sniff around the guys who would know, act like it's something I got a hand in. Give me a number to reach you if I get anything."

Gail scribbled on her card, which already had her cell number: "Darren Nakot/Anita Brown." Thanking Dre, she went on with her day taking the cup of coffee to go.

The same day Gail met with Dre in narcotics, the Steiner brothers were out prowling for victims. They had been to Loyola University a few times to attend clandestine skinhead meetings, usually late on a Saturday night. At least, that's what they thought of the meetings as; Nazi wannabes showed up and heard the rhetoric delivered by the speaker of the evening. The last meeting some woman spoke about the Asian threat; all these slant-eyed brainiacs taking over medicine in the United States. The Steiner brothers had no idea if this was the case, but it put them in a mood to do harm to any Asian they might come across.

It was late afternoon, and Sandy Chen, a young Vietnamese girl, was on her way to her job as a server at The Fifth Quarter, a sports bar where the college kids hung out to drink beer and watch football. Sten spotted her first; he almost always did because Steen had poor eyesight and had not had new glasses made in several years. Sten elbowed his brother saying, "Hey, would you look at that? A pretty little gook walking all by herself. Let's go show her a good time. They set off in pursuit of Chen, walking as fast as they could. Steen lumbered along, but he was too fat and soon had to stop to rest. Sten left him leaning on a building, following Chen to The Fifth Quarter. He wandered in and had a beer, watching as Sandy came on as a server and began her duties. He polished off the beer and found Sten where he had left him, just standing like a dog waiting for a command. Three nights later they came back, with a cloth hood and zip ties. Sten dropped a hood over her head, and they hauled her down an alley behind a dumpster, where they raped her on a large cardboard box they had flattened. Sten banged her head a couple of times on the pavement with the hood still over her head to disorient her. They took the hood and left her lying naked from the waist down on the flattened box. A man taking out the trash found her half an hour later. The cops were called and a rape kit was done at the hospital, but she could not give them any description of her attackers.

Thirty-three

Over the next month Decker made phone calls, took meetings with the parents and members of the Carnival Court, and knocked on every door he could think of. He found most of the parents to be pretty much as he expected. For the most part, they were good people who were a tad too self-important. He often got tears on both subjects, the death of Alisha and the temple massacre. Other than the flicker in Roe Stilton's eyes, he did not see or sense any connection to the temple shooting. He was certain Stilton was knocked off balance for a split second when he mentioned Temple Chabad. He felt like there was something there, but he had bubkes—zilch, nada, nothing. He could not go to his bosses and say, "I saw a flicker of something, I don't know what, when I mentioned the mass murder at the temple." They would think he was on drugs himself. Honestly, he could scarcely blame them if such flimsy flotsam was brought to their attention.

From the female members of the court, he learned a few things. To a person, they all felt there was some jealousy by Jenna of Alisha. That was long-standing, going back to childhood. Yet none of them knew or even suspected Jenna in any way. They seemed to regard the death as some type of terrible accident, although they had no idea how it might have occurred. Not a single male or female member of the court had seen anything out of the ordinary, either leading up to or during the ball. They all told a very similar tale of going as a group to University Hospital, save for Jenna, Ross Wilbanks, and the doctor who was in the court and followed the ambulance. They were sure none of those three were involved; the actions by each were nothing to raise eyebrows. The only thing that bothered Decker a bit was his inability to interview Jenna Dupreaux. She had been out of town in Los Angeles for most of this time. The reason was legit: She was on assignment by her TV station to monitor one of the female anchors and see what she could bring back to use locally. It was convenient for her in the sense of avoiding Decker. On the other hand, it was the way life was. Things happened that were beyond control. He had long ago learned to deal with the vicissitudes one encountered in police work. Finding himself a bit lost on both cases, with nothing to show for his effort, Decker decided to go back to the beginning. If the first round of interviews turned up nothing, go back and do them again.

His first was with the Bondurants. He had kept them up to speed as best he could, without revealing things of a confidential nature. Decker knew that time often allowed thoughts and memories to crystallize in the mind. When he called the Bondurants, Aline took his call. She was nearly breathless when she spoke. He feared she might hyperventilate. She sounded light-headed, in a reedy voice saying, "Mr. O'Day, Detective. ... Sorry, Detective O'Day, please tell me you have some news?"

Decker heard the pain in her voice, replying, "Mrs. Bondurant, please call me Decker. Unfortunately, I have nothing new. I'm so sorry, I wish I knew more. That's why I'm calling. I've spoken to everyone except Jenna Dupreaux. She's out of town, on assignment. So I'm starting over. I intend to reinterview everyone. I was hoping I could come by and speak with you and Mr. Bondurant."

Aline gasped, and Decker heard sniffling. She composed herself and replied, "Detective ... Decker. Hunt is in China for two weeks on business. I was hoping for more. What's this about Jenna Dupreaux?"

Decker told her what he knew, saying he had been unable to speak with her. He heard Aline clear her throat, then she continued, "Yes, I can't say I'm surprised. Jenna is a slippery one, always has been."

"What do you mean, slippery one?" Decker replied. "No one has mentioned any suspicions about her. Do you know something? Please tell me, no matter how trivial."

Silence for thirty seconds followed. Then Aline said, "All her life Jenna has been the main attraction. The exception was Alisha. She could not keep the pace with Alisha. Pardon my saying so, but Alisha was prettier. She bested Jenna in academics. Jenna went to LSU; Alisha won a scholarship to UVA. Jenna was popular for sure, but Alisha was a star, Detective. Do you understand what I'm saying?"

Decker answered, "Yes, okay. Is there more?"

"Yes, just a few odds and ends. I'll have to talk to some friends, get their recollections. Things happened as the girls grew up. I know there were several involving Jenna. I'll get the details and get back to you. The one I remember vividly happened at our church. The girls were eleven or twelve at the time. As they went downstairs to Sunday school, one boy fell. I believe he broke an arm and had damage to his teeth. Alisha saw it happen. She swore Jenna caused it on purpose. Of course, Jenna cried and denied it. Her parents took her side, as they always did. But Alisha was adamant. It was no accident to her. I never knew Alisha to lie about anything, so I have no reason to doubt what she saw. I recognize that the girls were young, and her perception could have been inaccurate. But she was sure. Do you understand, Detective?"

"Huh. Okay, Mrs. Bondurant, see what else you can dig up. First I've heard of that. Long time ago, but still ... huh."

"I'll be in touch, Detec—, Decker. Thank you so much for staying on this. I know there is something there. I feel it as a mother. Goodbye, Decker."

Decker stood thinking. He was puzzled. Nothing to make a big deal out of, but still ... odd. Huh, he thought.

Thirty-four

The Steiner brothers stood on top of the overpass where I-10 crossed above North Claiborne Street. They were scouting; their current obsession was to kill a Black person; it did not matter who, just anyone would do. They had heard of kids dropping things from an overpass on cars passing below. Sten thought that was cool; drop a rock or something heavy from the overpass and book it. No fuss, no muss; no confrontation with the chance of someone identifying them in a chance encounter. And the best part was they could wear gloves, so no prints. Just boom, right down on the car, and they'd be gone before anyone knew what happened. Sten was by nature a coward, slight of build and picked on from birth. He was meaner that a junkyard dog and was constantly high on meth if he had money. Today was no different. They were both jacked up from a hit of meth and stood watching cars pass below them on North Claiborne. Steen, who was a bit slow, said, "Dude, you really gonna drop some shit on a car from up here? Man, that'll be something. Are we gonna kill a nigger?"

"Damn right, bro. We gonna get us one. Look at 'em, driving along down there, and we ain't even got a car. Damn welfare gives 'em money that ought to be ours. I aim to drop a concrete block right through the windshield of some coon passing under here. Teach 'em a lesson, ya know?"

Steen was puzzled. "What lesson? What they gon' learn from that?"

"You idiot. I don't mean they'll really learn anything. What I mean is we'll teach 'em they gotta be careful, watch their damn step. Maybe put a scare in 'em. Yeah, that'll be good, scare their sorry asses."

Two days later they were back on the overpass. This time they had gloves on, and Steen was lugging a concrete block. He complained bitterly, but Sten was the brains of the outfit and he was the brawn. They kept their backs to passing cars, thinking they could not be identified if no one saw their faces. Sten smoked a cigarette, watching for the right car. Eventually, he saw a small Hyundai approaching at slow speed, a Black woman driving. He flicked the cigarette butt away and said, "Steen, get your ass over here with that block. When I say now, you drop that sumbitch. Ready?" Steen nodded, and as the car approached Sten yelled, "Now." The block fell directly into the windshield and smashed straight through. Sten let out a whoop, high-fived his brother, and they hurried away. Sten had no way of knowing the damage, but he was sure the woman was hurt. Fuck her, he thought, the Black bitch.

Thirty-five

Decker was at his desk making appointments for reinterviews with the parents of court members when Double L hurried over. He spoke rapidly. "Decker, get over the 10 overpass above North Claiborne Avenue. Dispatch just got a call that someone dropped a cinder block off the overpass and killed a woman. I need you there now. Everybody else is out in the streets."

Decker hurried to his Mustang and set the flashers up top. He plugged them in, hit the gas, and sped off to North Claiborne Avenue where the overpass of I-10 crossed it. He got there twenty minutes later, finding a couple of cruisers on either side of the underpass. They had the road blocked off, and Decker saw a Kia that had run off the road and hit a power pole. He jumped out and hustled over to the Kia. He could see the broken windshield and a woman's body inside. The closest officer saw him coming, and Decker flashed the shield, saying, "Detective O'Day. What the hell happened?"

The cop, whose name tag read Saunders, replied, "Someone called it in. The caller said she'd seen two males up on the 10 overpass drop a block as she drove past. She knew to call it in but really had no details. She went by too fast to see much. Probably about 85, which is the unwritten speed limit here in New Orleans. We roll up and find the victim in her car, dead as a doornail. Head's all bashed in. We felt for a pulse, but there was no chance. The fuckin' block nearly knocked her head clean off. Waiting for the ME. My partner made that call. No idea who this lady is."

"Thanks. Good work, Saunders. Keep the lookie-loos away. I'm gonna head up top and see if I see anything up there. Holler when the ME gets here."

"Will do, sir," the young patrolman replied. Decker made his way around the fence below the overpass and climbed the embankment. Getting to the top, he walked along the side of the highway onto the bridge. Cars flew by, and Decker was a little concerned that someone might be texting and run him down. Not seeing anything obvious, he decided to head back down and call for some units to close one lane of traffic so they could safely process the overpass as a crime scene. The ME arrived and pronounced the woman dead. Criminalists rolled up a few minutes later, and Decker spent the next four hours on scene. They scoured the overpass but found nothing other than a cigarette butt that looked fresh. They bagged it, and Decker cleared the scene at five minutes until six o'clock.

The senseless death angered Decker deeply; it was depressing. A woman had died a violent death, the random victim of a malicious act. It was a total disregard for human life, and Decker wondered what drove someone to do such a thing as hurl a cinder block off an overpass at a motorist passing below? He thought it was a random act, but he was wrong. He had no way of knowing at that moment that this was a hate crime. Decker often went to the boxing gym to work off his anger and depression. He drove directly to Resolve when he left the crime scene. It was his second appearance of the day. He'd sparred that morning at 6:00. Now he gloved up and went after the heavy bag with a vengeance. His ferocity was noticed by others in the gym. Cleve, one of the guys who worked there at night, passed the word: "Stay clear of Decker tonight. He's in a mood to hurt someone." Cleve was spot on. If Decker could have found them that night, he'd have beaten the assholes that dropped the block to death. He had to settle for the heavy bag, which took a real pounding.

Thirty-six

One week after Decker spoke with Aline Bondurant she called him and invited him to drop by after breakfast the next day. He boxed, cleaned up, ate a protein bar, and headed over to the Bondurant house. He pulled up at 8:15. Aline Bondurant answered the door herself, inviting him to the breakfast nook overlooking a garden. Decker saw many types of beautiful flowers, most of which he knew nothing about. He complimented her on the garden, and her response was that it kept her busy and she enjoyed the process as much as the flowers. The maid brought coffee for them both, and Aline got down to business. "Sorry it took so long. Reaching back over the time is a bit challenging. Memories fade, people move, that kind of thing. I did learn a couple things that may interest you."

"Fine," Decker responded. "Fire away."

Aline began. "I chased down a friend who now lives in Houston. Her daughter attended the junior high school that Jenna Dupreaux attended. She remembered an incident from the eighth grade. It seems Jenna was accused of smoking marijuana by one of the teachers. A woman named Mitzi Carroll. The Carroll woman claimed that Jenna was behind the school smoking when she happened upon her. She smelled that smell of marijuana, according to my friend. She says it has an unmistakable smell."

Decker smiled, agreeing. "One sniff, and you know it forever."

"Apparently," she nodded. "Anyhow, the teacher confronted Jenna and Jenna ate the ... nub. She had a name for it."

"A roach," Decker responded. "That's what the butt end is called."

"Yes, she ate the roach. Just popped it into her mouth, and it was gone. The teacher filed a report accusing Jenna, and the school was considering disciplinary action, possibly expulsion. It was a very good school, high standards. So, shortly thereafter vile pornography was discovered in the teacher's desk. Supposedly the janitor was cleaning and saw something sticking out of the bottom drawer. He opened it to push the object into the drawer and bang ... a whole bunch of lewd pictures are scattered about. He reported that, and the teacher was let go shortly thereafter. My friend said there were questions about the whole affair. The janitor got a new truck about two months later, and the case against Jenna was dropped. At the end of the term Jenna moved to a new school, and that was that."

Decker listened and then asked, "So, you're telling me that some folks thought it was a frame job, and the janitor was paid off. Is that about right?"

"Exactly. You'd have to know the Dupreaux family to really understand the dynamics. Hunt says the father is a pompous ass with a lot of family money. He's smart, according to Hunt, but his ethics are very questionable. As for Suzanne Dupreaux, she's a bitch, pardon me for saying so. She thinks the world spins just for her and Jenna. They have protected Jenna, shielded her all her life. When Jenna was a freshman at LSU another really bad rumor made the rounds. The rumor was that Jenna had a female lover. The girl in question committed suicide. The rumor mill had it that Jenna had something to do with it. Once again, photographs were involved. Word was that the young woman discovered that someone had posted nude photos of her on a website and sent the link to every fraternity on campus. This young woman dropped out of school and ended up killing herself a few months later. All this was rumor, mind you. No proof of anything and of course Jenna denied every-thing. Her parents whisked her off to Europe that summer, and it all blew over. The girl's parents blamed Jenna, and part of the rumor was the Dupreauxs bought them off to make it go away."

Decker considered all this before speaking. When he did, he said, "Mrs. Bondurant, these are pretty serious allega-tions. Are your sources credible? What I'm asking is, are you just a grieving mother looking for someone to blame? Or do you think these things have legs, actually happened the way you describe them?"

Aline countered immediately. "The incident in junior high school happened. My friend is certain of that. Her daughter did not like Jenna and said all the girls believed Jenna was involved. They knew she smoked marijuana. The rest is just what everyone thought, but my friend said the janitor got a new truck for sure. The LSU incident is a little more tenuous. Alisha was at UVA, and all that I told you came from the country club bridge group. The ladies play cards and drink wine. I can't say it happened that way, but I can tell you I heard versions of the story from multiple sources, none of whom are known liars."

"If what you've told me is true, Jenna is a devious young woman. Her parents are enablers, and they have no qualms about protecting Jenna."

Aline nodded her agreement, saying, "That is exactly what I'm telling you. I have no proof Jenna has done a thing. She is clever and devious. From my perspective, she's a bit off. I'm no psychiatrist, but all her life things have happened and other people got hurt in some fashion. Jenna always came out smelling like a rose. I suppose what it all comes down to is, I don't trust that girl. Alisha was Queen, and Jenna made no secret she wanted to be the Queen of Carnival. Now Alisha is dead; I'm left wondering what happened and why. That's all I know, Decker."

Decker was about to stand up, but one more thought popped into his head. "What do you know about the Stiltons, Mrs. Bondurant? What sort of people are they?"

Aline considered her words and then spoke. "Roe Stilton is a little bigot. He hates everything and everyone that is not lily White. It's well known in our circles. Not many like him, and his son is a bit of a ne'er-do-well, lives on Daddy's money. Does drugs, according to the kids. That's all I know."

"Thank you very much, Mrs. Bondurant. This is all very interesting; it may be helpful. I'll keep looking."

"Goodbye, Decker. Thanks for keeping me in the loop. Please keep working Alisha's death. It's all that keeps me going."

Thirty-seven

Jenna was an eighth grader in full puberty when Mrs. Carroll caught her smoking a joint in the parking lot. She had thought she was safe enough. It was lunchtime, and the parking lot was deserted. She'd done it before with no problem. But today Mrs. Carroll had come out to her car to retrieve her wallet, which she had left in her car that morning. She was alone and did not expect to see anyone, but as she approached her car she caught the odor of marijuana. She quietly walked to the next row of cars and peeked around an SUV. Jenna Dupreaux was sitting on the bumper of a truck two vehicles down, smoking a joint. No question in Mrs. Carroll's mind. They'd had the NOPD officer visit and give the talk on drugs, complete with samples and what to look for. He'd even burned a trace of weed, as he called it, for them to know the smell.

Mrs. Carroll stepped into view, saying, "Jenna, I want that ... thing right now." Jenna popped the rest of the joint into her mouth and swallowed it. "What are you talking about?" she responded, a smirk on her face.

Mrs. Carroll could hardly believe it, ordering Jenna to come with her. "We are going to the principal's office right now. I can't believe you ate that thing. It was lit, for heaven's sake."

Jenna shook her head. "I didn't eat anything, and I'm not going to the office. You tell anybody anything, and I'll deny it. It'll be your word against mine." With that Jenna turned and ran off toward the school. Mrs. Carroll was stunned but made her way to Mr. Dickey's office and reported the incident. Dickey summoned Jenna to the office, where she promptly denied it and said Mrs. Carroll had it in for her. She started to cry and ask for her mother. Suzanne Dupreaux showed up half an hour later demanding to see her daughter. She denied that Jenna would do such a thing and took Jenna home. As principal, Mr. Dickey had to report it to the school's disciplinary board for review. The matter was put on the agenda for the following month.

At the Dupreaux house, Suzanne was more concerned with how it would look to her friends than whether Jenna had actually smoked weed. If Jenna was found guilty by the review board, she would likely be suspended or expelled. That would stain her record, as well the Dupreaux family. For her part, Jenna continued to deny it all, and Suzanne hectored her husband daily, saying, "Do something, damn it. We must protect Jenna. It'll ruin her life." Patrick was not convinced that Suzanne was correct, but he knew he would never hear the end of it unless he did something.

A few days before the disciplinary board was to meet, a janitor, Tee Lewis, happened to open a desk drawer in Mrs. Carroll's desk, where he reported finding child pornography of the most vile kind. He took the magazines to the office and handed them over to Mr. Dickey. Mrs. Carroll vehemently denied knowing anything about the magazines, but Lewis stuck to his story and her reputation was destroyed. With the sole accuser under fire and likely to lose her job, the disciplinary board dismissed the case against Jenna. At the end of the school year, Mrs. Carroll was asked to leave and Jenna transferred. Suzanne and Jenna celebrated with a trip to New York and a shopping spree. Jenna was blossoming, certain she was the cat's meow. Suzanne, of course, told everyone who would listen how shabbily Jenna had been treated and how glad they were to be going to a new high school.

Thirty-eight

Jenna was in a bit of a state. She was proud of herself for seducing Win Bentley. That had promise for her future in wealth acquisition. She'd nailed him good. It would take him a couple of days to recover. She had literally rubbed him raw. But his mentioning fentanyl and a cop poking around freaked her out a little. She knew there were no witnesses. They would have surfaced by now. She'd known an autopsy was inevitable and a tox report was a certainty. Still, hearing it spoken aloud following Win's interview with a cop made her nervous. She needed to think. When she really needed to think she popped a Vistaril and listened to music in her bedroom. She had a nice sound system, and she put on some soothing jazz instrumentals. She lay down on her bed, dimmed the lights, and tried to relax and think.

The drug took effect after awhile and she was calmer, more in a Zen state. Okay, the cops were sniffing around. Was there any link back to her? She did not think so, certainly not a direct link. The only connection was Dare. Dare was her supplier of drugs as well as her lover. Dare did not know she had killed Alisha. She'd told no one, careful as always. Dare was engaged in criminal activity too, so he was very unlikely to have much to do with the cops. Dare also had a little secret that only Jenna knew about. The previous year she had let herself in to Dare's place late one night. She often used a penlight so she did not trip over something in the dark lying on his floor. What she found that night was a pretty Black girl, naked on the floor and out cold. She knew Dare had lots of lovers coming through his door, but on this night it just hit Jenna wrong. She got angry. No, she got more than angry. She got blindingly angry. The girl was partially covered by a blanket, and Dare was nowhere in sight. She figured Dare had given the girl a roofie and had sex with her once she was zonked. She crept to his bedroom door and peeked in. He was out; she figured he had chemicals in his system too. Without really thinking it through, Jenna went to his kitchen and got a straw. He kept a box for blow and for sipping Tab, his drink of choice. She knew where he kept his stash of blow and retrieved it. She put the baggie down, stuffed the end of a straw with coke, and blew it up the girl's nose. She did the same to the other nostril. She did this several times and eventually the girl started to thrash wildly, then stopped moving. She never woke up, and Jenna sat transfixed watching it happen. She put a finger under the girl's nose and felt no breath. Dead as a stone. Let Dare find that on the floor in the morning. She did not think the cops would look for DNA up the girl's nostrils. She pocketed the straw, put Dare's stash back, and let herself out.

Jenna worked it through in her mind; she had a big tool to leverage Dare should push come to shove. She could always drop a dime on Dare if need be. But she was still worried that he might under pressure tell the cops he had given her fentanyl. That was her only weak spot, at least that she could see. No reason to act now. She liked Dare, and he was a good fuck. No disputing that. The drugs were a bonus. Just something to keep in mind if things got hairy. She did not relish the idea of killing Dare, but if it came to her welfare, it was a no-brainer. Satisfied with her mental dissection of the matter, she fell asleep, completely relaxed.

Thirty-nine

Occasionally in police work the cops catch a real break. Decker was in his car when Bluetooth intercepted a call and put it to his car speakers. He hit answer, and the dispatch came on the line. "Detective, I have a man who claims he has information on the homicide on North Claiborne. Can I put him through?"

"Do it," Decker replied.

A new voice came over the speakers. "Detective?"

"Yes, this is Decker O'Day. Who am I speaking with?"

"My name's Acuff, Ben Acuff."

"How can I help you, Mr. Acuff? Do you know something about the murder on North Claiborne?"

The man responded: "On the news last night I saw that business about the lady killed by a cinder block thrown from the overpass. I was driving by over that bridge two days ago, and I seen two guys I recognized. These dudes were looking off the overpass down on North Claiborne. I thought it was odd, them being up there. They weren't doing nothing, just looking. Then I seen the news last night. It clicked, ya know? These guys I seen … bad news. The Steiner brothers. They got to be involved."

Decker asked, "Did you see their faces? How do you know it was them?"

"Easy. One's a big tub of lard, about six foot three. The other is a shrimp, maybe five foot five with his boots on. I seen their jackets and clothing. These dudes are skinheads. They run around all the time wearing these black motorcycle jackets with a swastika embroidered in red on the back. Exactly what I seen. Big and Little with these jackets with the swastikas. Didn't have to see faces. They might as well've had on a neon sign with their names. Dumb fucks, always mouthing about Jews and niggers and how they're gonna get them one. Now I guess they did!"

Decker could hardly believe his good fortune. He asked Acuff, "Where do these mutts hang out? Where do you see 'em?"

"Sally's Balls, a pool room down by the Quarter. I shoot a few games there time to time. They're always in there, talking shit and bitching about the niggers and Jews."

Decker thanked him and told him he'd send a cop around to take a statement. Acuff said he had given dispatch his contact information and would give a full statement to whoever came by. Decker turned left at the next light and headed for the Quarter. He asked Siri for directions to Sally's Balls. He got there about 6:15, parking down the street. He checked his gun, a Glock 30 45 ACP, which he carried in a leather holster clipped to his belt at the small of his back. He went to his trunk and slipped off his loafers, opting for steel-toed work boots. He headed to the pool hall. As soon as he stepped through the door, he saw Ice, the dealer whose nose he'd broken earlier. Ice still had bandages across his nose but smiled at Decker, saying, "Boys, I smell pork. This pig busted my nose awhile back. Let's give him a nice welcome."

Decker scanned the room, noting a Nazi flag on the wall. A large skinhead with a leather vest and swastikas on his arms came around the counter where the cash register was. "I'm Sally. We don't allow hog shit in here, boy." A skinny, longhaired guy who looked like a biker stopped his game and took a step forward, rotating his cue stick to put the big end away from his hands.

Decker did not hesitate. He pulled the Glock from the small of his back and racked a round into the chamber. "Put the stick down, rat face. I'm happy to put a 45 slug in your chest if you don't. I'm looking for the Steiner brothers. They around?" Rat face put the stick back in its place.

Ice said, "Fuck you. You a real tough dude with that gun, ain't ya?"

Decker sighed, and put the gun back in his holster. "Ice, you dickweeds are all the same. Dumber than a box of rocks. Didn't that broken nose teach you any manners?" Sally, the biggest of the three, charged him. Decker expected it, knowing that Ice was mostly talk and rat face was too far away to be an immediate threat. Decker took a false step to his left to change Sally's direction, then took two short, quick boxing steps the other direction. As Sally lumbered past, Decker drove his heel into the side of Sally's knee, a perfect front kick. The knee blew out and Sally crashed to the floor screaming. Decker never slowed, pulling a set of brass knuckles from his pocket. No reason to bust a knuckle on these meatheads. The knuckles had belonged to his father, Aidan. His uncle Gil swore they originally belonged to their father, Ian O'Day, who won them in a card game on the boat bringing him to America. Decker was a bit doubtful about their origin, but they were definitely his dad's. They were with his uniform and personal items delivered in a box after his death. They even had AD scratched into them.

He was on rat face before the man could retrieve his cue stick, driving the brass knuckles into the man's jaw. He heard bone break, felt the facial bones yield. Rat face went down, and he turned to Ice. Ice had pulled a big hunting knife from his back, and Decker dropped the brass knuckles. He grabbed a pool cue and swung low, catching Ice right above the knee on the outside of his leg. The big nerve there controls the leg and instantly shot pain through Ice's body. The leg stopped working. Ice tried to remain standing, but the leg gave out, and he fell to the floor. Decker thought about hitting him with the cue stick again but decided he had made his point. He looked down at Ice, saying quietly,

"Tell the Steiner brothers I'm looking for them. Tell 'em if I have to come find 'em they'll be in the hospital for a while. You got that, Ice?"

Ice was holding his leg, in obvious agony. Through gritted teeth he hissed, "Yeah, okay. Just don't hit me no more." Decker wiped the pool cue for fingerprints and set it back in the rack. He picked up his brass knuckles, wiping them on rat face's shirt. He left the way he came in. Only later did he see the dried blood spatter on his shirt from hitting rat face with the knuckles. He dropped the shirt in a dumpster on his way home and rode with the window open and no shirt.

Forty

ail Waites was furious. She was interviewing a fourteen-year-old Black girl named June Greene. June was sitting in the chair next to Gail's desk in the sex crimes unit. She was drinking from a bottle of cold water Gail had pulled from the mini refrigerator outside her captain's office. June had barely escaped becoming a rape victim several hours earlier. She was still plenty shaken but ready to tell Gail her story. June took a long pull from the bottle as she began. "Ms. Gail, I didn't do anything wrong. Why did they pick on me?"

Gail had no good answer, so she gave her stock answer. "Honey, it ain't got nothin' to do with you. It's about power and control for guys who rape. They got a screw or two loose. Now, tell me exactly what happened."

June nodded, beginning, "You know my mother teaches at Loyola, in the music department. She has a late class, runs from 6:30 until 7:30 in the evening. I walk over to campus from school and hang out, do my homework. Sometimes I sit through Mama's class and then we go home. Tonight I was hungry and restless. I'd just left the Music Center and was headed to the cafeteria. Next thing I know some ape is trying to pull something over my head, over my eyes. He was big, I could tell that even though he was behind me. I bumped into him as he jerked me backwards, and I hit his chin with the back of my head. I guess it stunned him a little because he turned loose for just a second. That was all I needed. I took off fast as I could. I run sprints in track so I'm pretty quick out of the blocks. I ran just like that, like I was coming out of the blocks and accelerating. Another guy tried to grab my arm, but he was a shrimp. I ran right through that. Guess I was so scared I had a little extra strength."

Gail said, "Honey, you did great. You got away. Now, did you see faces? Were they Black or White?"

"White for sure. I saw hands, not faces. It was too dark. But one was big, over six feet, and fat. He felt flabby when I bumped his stomach. The other guy, I think, yelled something as I ran off. The small, shrimpy guy. I couldn't quite make it out, and I was hauling. It sounded like 'She a' or 'She's a,' something like that. I never looked back and didn't slow down until I was in the room with my mother. I just busted into the middle of her class. I was so scared, just shaking. Things are fuzzy from there. Everybody in class jumped up. They called the campus police. That's all I can tell you."

Gail spoke gently. "June, you did great. You really did. I'll find these guys. You've given me a description. White, one large and the other short. There have been two rapes in the last nine months close to the Loyola campus. Neither of those girls were able to give us anything. They were grabbed from behind, had their head covered so they couldn't see. Both raped and sodomized. You were very brave and very lucky you were not a victim too. I'll walk you and your mother out to your car. June, be very careful. I'll find these guys now that I have something to work with. Until I do, watch yourself. Don't leave the Music Center. They're operating close to Loyola, maybe live nearby or go to school there. Better safe than sorry until I get ahold of these mutts."

Forty-one

Gail saw the BOLO (be on the lookout) for the Steiner brothers. She immediately noticed the description: White, one large and fat, one small, approximately five foot five, both wearing jackets with swastikas. Her mind flashed to the description given by June Greene, and she felt a charge she got when she was onto something. She was looking for two rapists who matched that physical description almost to a T. How many could there be? No cop believed in coincidences, especially where shitbirds were involved. She reached for the phone, calling Detective O'Day, who was listed as the requesting officer. Decker picked up on the second ring. "Detective O'Day."

"Detective, this is Gail Waites in sex crimes. I'm working some rape cases, and I'm looking at your BOLO. I'm thinking we're looking for the same two assholes. Can we meet?"

"Absolutely," Decker responded. "Where are you?"

"I'm at the Broad Street Station," Gail replied.

"I'm working out of the Tulane Police Department temporarily. How about you come over, and I'll buy you a cup of coffee. Deal?" Decker asked.

"I'm on my way," Gail headed for her car. Driving over she could not stop thinking about Anita Brown, her lifeless body dumped on Tulane Avenue. She could see no connection with these mooks, but she had been a cop long enough to know you often found manna from heaven in the strangest places. She figured she'd talk with O'Day, then swing by and say hi to Jean at University. She pulled to a stop at Tulane PD a few minutes later and went inside. She was directed to O'Day's desk, where he was pressing his cell to his ear. He saw her and held up one finger. He ended his call and stood, extending his hand.

"Decker O'Day," he said warmly.

"I'm Gail Waites. Thanks for seeing me."

Decker said, "Follow me," and led her to a coffee urn where they both fixed coffee. He then led her back to his desk and yanked a chair from a nearby table. Gail got right to business. "You're looking for the Steiner brothers?"

"Yep. They're my main suspects in the death of the Kinlaw woman on North Claiborne, below the 10 overpass."

Gail continued, "Well, last night I took a description from a fourteen-year-old girl that fit your BOLO. Two White guys tried to grab her over at Loyola. Her mother's a music teacher there. She did not see faces in the dark, but the physical description matches your BOLO. What do you know about these assholes?"

Decker smiled, saying, "Assholes for sure. One's a big lard-ass; his brother is small, wiry, maybe five foot five in high heels. The fucks dropped a cinder block and killed the Kinlaw woman as she was driving home from work. I have a witness who saw those two on the overpass two days before. Did not see faces, but he knows them from around. Says they hate Blacks and Jews, always in biker jackets with red swastikas on the back. Did your girl see anything like that?"

"No, but I'm betting it's them. She felt the fat dude's flabby belly when he pulled her backwards. Hit the back of her head on his chin, and he let go, just for a second. That's what saved her. She took off like a scalded dog. Other short dude tried to grab her arm, but she was too fast and too scared. She knows the fat guy was tall because she only came up to his chin and she's a tall drink of water. Two other girls raped near the Loyola campus in the past nine months. Got rape kits from both, but I'm not sure they've been processed. Backlog and budget cuts, what can you do?"

Decker shook his head in frustration, saying, "It's absurd. Why we can't get DNA money to take some of these animals off the street is beyond me. It sure sounds like the same two guys, though. I, ah … chatted with some of their friends last night. My guess is they'll be lying low, avoiding me. I promised them some hospital time if they didn't come see me."

Decker watched Gail break into a smile for the first time: "Chatted, huh. Yeah, I bet you did. I know your name. Boxing from a few years ago, am I right?"

Decker smiled back. "Guilty."

Gail then responded. "I get to these shitbirds first, I may bust a cap in their ass. I do not play with these types."

"Yeah, they're mutts. Skinhead types, at least that's what it seems to me. Swastikas on their jackets. Their pals hang in a pool hall named Sally's Balls. Nazi flag on the wall. Definitely neo-Nazi kinds of guys. I am puzzled by one thing: Why would assholes like that be hanging around Loyola? It's a Catholic University. No way these mooks are students. I'm not seeing any connection, ya know?"

Gail nodded in agreement, responding, "Good question. I'm heading that way later today. I'll ask the girl's mother if she has any ideas. Dickheads like them, I may get lucky. They may be standing on a street corner as I roll by, swastika jackets and all. If so, I may pull a drive-by!" she said laughing. Decker laughed too.

"Fine by me. Just make sure you hit what you're aiming for and keep going. Fuck a bunch of DNA testing." They both laughed at that idea. Gail left and Decker went back to his laptop.

Forty-two

Gail left her meeting with Decker. She swung by University and saw Jean Brown for a moment, reassuring her that she was still looking for answers on Anita. She told Jean she would be home late and not to wait on her for supper. She then went back to the Broad Street Station and got busy with her daily reports, review, phone calls, and the like. She had a meeting set with June Greene and her mother at 5:00 that afternoon at Loyola. She left in time to fight her way over through end of the day traffic. She parked and met them in the school cafeteria as they had agreed. June's mother, Lucille Greene, was still very shaken by her daughter's ordeal. Gail assured her that she had a good lead on the two men, although she was not free to give out their names. June seemed to be handling it better than her mother, at ease and drinking a glass of green tea. Gail knew that her appearance might belie her true emotions. She also knew the shock might hit home later, when least expected.

Gail started off by giving them a sort of canned talk about dealing with a crime from the victim's perspective. She supplied a counselor's name and suggested that June and Lucille attend some counseling. They listened intently and agreed to explore counseling. Gail gave them another card with her cell number, telling them to call day or night. That was well and good, but they really wanted an update on the perpetrators.

Gail knew that was coming, responding, "I can't give you names. I can tell you I feel pretty good about who these two guys are. I had a meeting this morning with a detective in a different division. He's looking for two guys in another beef.

The physical description of these guys is a match, at least in body type. These guys are most likely skinheads. Nazi types with swastikas and a load of hate on for Black folks. He's hot on their trail, and now I am too. It's a matter of time before we find these jacklegs and haul their butts in. That is, unless they skip town. Either way, the heat is on, and we think they'll be lying low. I don't think you guys are really in danger. My feeling is June was a victim of opportunity, not a target they were stalking. I don't know that for a fact, but everything about this case and their other beef says random."

Lucille let out a huge sigh, saying, "Thank you, Jesus. I was afraid these monsters had locked onto June for some reason. But it doesn't sound that way. You mentioned some other attacks last night, but that was a blur. What about those?"

Gail responded, "Random, we think. Those two rapes were several months apart and other than rape kits, we've had nothing to go on. No description, car, nothing. The only common thing I've been able to see is that those attacks took place close to Loyola. June was on campus last night, but the others were close. Too close for me to think it coincidental. What I can't figure is why Loyola? Why would skinheads be hanging around a Catholic Jesuit College? Y'all got any ideas?"

June shook her head no, and Lucille spoke, saying, "That's just weird. Why indeed? Most of our students are good kids from Catholic families. I'm at a loss on why Nazis would be hanging around here? In my time here I've not seen any of that type ... skinheads. Or if I did, I failed to recognize them as such. Gail, you're talking about the kind of guys you see at rallies on the news, swastikas, shaved heads, Nazi flags, the whole bit, right?"

"Yes, exactly. It's got me stumped. The detective said these two go about in leather jackets with red swastikas embroidered on the back of the jackets. One a big tub of lard, tall, like well over six feet. The other a short wiry guy. The kind of guys who would stand out like flashing signs around here; no way you could miss them."

Lucille spoke next, saying, "We'll keep our eyes open, that's for sure. June, you see anybody matches either of those descriptions, you put those long legs to use and don't stop running until you get to the Loyola PD or inside with other people who can protect you. You hear me?"

"Yes, Mama. Don't you worry. I'm not letting anybody get close to me. I thought I was safe here on campus; that was a false sense of security. I've learned my lesson. I'll be real careful, I promise."

"Good," Lucille replied. "Gail, I'll ask around and do a bit of research. See if I can find something that might draw bottom feeders to Loyola. It's a fine school; it's been great for me. If I learn anything I'll call you. Thank you again for being there for us. Good luck catching these losers. Be careful, girl, you're Black too, ya know?"

Gail stood and patted her duty weapon. "I know. Believe me, I know. Guys like this do not want to see me coming. Especially not with Miss Boom cocked and locked on my hip." She said goodbye and headed for her car. It had been a long but good day.

Forty-three

Decker was finally able to schedule an interview with Jenna Dupreaux two months after Alisha's death. He wanted to gain her trust, not wanting to spook her. She sounded open and friendly over the phone, suggesting they meet after work at Bijou Bar and Restaurant. It was on North Rampart Street, near WWL, where she worked. Decker was there at 6:00. Five minutes later a cute blond girl with pigtails came in and headed in his direction in the bar. He stood, extended his hand, introducing himself. "I'm Decker O'Day. Thanks for meeting with me."

Jenna shook his hand, holding on for just a second too long. She smiled a big smile, saying, "Nice to meet you, Detective. I'm Jenna Dupreaux. Please call me Jenna."

Decker responded, "Do you prefer the bar or a table?"

She replied, "How about a booth? I'm tired. My day started early."

"Of course," he replied. They asked for a booth and were soon seated with drinks. She had wine, and he had a Pale Ale.

Jenna looked at him, took a sip of wine, and said, "I'm still in shock. I cannot believe Alisha is gone."

"Unfortunately, she is. You two knew each other a long time; that's what I've been told."

"Like, forever," Jenna said. "I mean, we were just kids growing up together. Maybe back to preschool with Mrs. Betty, I think. I ... ah, God, I ..." Tears flowed freely down Jenna's cheeks. She put her napkin to her face and sobbed. Decker sat quietly, watching. If this was an act, Decker thought, she was good, really good. At length she seemed to right herself and had another sip of wine. "So unfair, just not right. Queen of Rex ... what happened, Decker?"

It was subtle, but now he was Decker, not Detective. He answered, "A fentanyl overdose killed Alisha. I'm trying to put it all together."

She jumped back in. "So, is this like, a murder investigation? Did someone kill Alisha?"

Decker could not quite get over the pigtails. Jenna was a grown woman, but her pigtails and look of innocence made her seem about seventeen. He knew she was not, of course, but the look was pure: a sad little girl who had lost a childhood friend. He replied, "We don't know. That's my job, to figure out what really happened that night. Was it an accident? A suicide? Or did someone take her life? I need you to help me with my inquiry."

"Oh, of course," she purred. "I'll do anything I can. Let me tell you what I remember." For the next forty-five minutes, Jenna described her day in great detail. She remembered exactly where she had been, the time, the people she saw, right down to the time of Alisha's death. She told of leaving the ball early, having a migraine, and going straight to bed. Her ability to recall the slightest details was truly remarkable.

When she wound down, Decker asked, "Where were you when you first heard Alisha was down?"

Without hesitation she replied, "I was with Mr. Russell. I remember, I'd just gotten a drink. Someone, a lady, I think, came over and told us Alisha had ... collapsed. I'm sure that's what she said. I bet Mr. Russell will remember if you ask him. We were on the opposite side of the room, so I couldn't see anything. I know—was told—they took her out on a stretcher. I got the migraine soon afterwards and had Ross Wilbanks drive me straight home. He was my knight.

I learned the next morning that poor Alisha was dead. I haven't slept well since."

Decker nodded, soaking up her story. "Well, you were nowhere close when it happened. Did Alisha use drugs, Jenna?"

"I didn't think so. I never saw her take anything. I ... I guess now I'm not so sure. I mean, how else would she have gotten this stuff that killed her in her system?"

Decker gave her an honest answer. "I don't know. She certainly could have taken the fentanyl. Any idea where she might have gotten drugs if she used them?"

Jenna was all over that one. "Crawford. Crawford Stilton. He does drugs. I've seen him snort coke ... cocaine at a party before. He would know where to get something like that."

Decker nodded, saying, "Yeah, I've heard drugs are part of his thing. You've never done any drugs have you, Jenna?"

"Heavens no, Decker. I'm a fraidy-cat. I don't do any of that stuff. I don't. Not even weed." Bingo, Decker thought. He'd done his homework and talked with everyone he could about the junior high school incident. He'd even located and talked to the teacher who was fired. She was adamant that she was set up and fired because she reported Jenna for smoking marijuana. She pointed to her track record since. She'd worked for years without a hiccup in the Atlanta school system. In and of itself, Decker had nothing. But he felt the first stirring in his gut. He looked at the pigtailed girl seated across from him and his lizard brain whispered, "Danger, danger, danger." They talked on for a while and eventually walked out together. Jenna gave his arm a squeeze right before she turned and walked away. "Uh-oh," he thought.

Forty-four

Within the sex crimes division, Gail Waites had been given the nickname Hammerhead. It arose from her go-to move in a fight: the head butt. Powerfully built, tall and strong, she wielded a legendary head butt. She had stumbled into the move as a child. Playing kickball one day in the Calliope, she charged forward to kick the ball. An older boy of fourteen surged from the opposite direction, and Gail's forehead struck him on the jaw. He crumpled, having suffered a significant concussion. Gail was twelve at the time and always in a fight to survive. She figured if it put that kid out of commission, it was worth a try on others. In the projects she had lots of opportunities to work on the move, and in time she had it down. No leaning backward to give warning. She had two versions, depending on her adversary. With those in her general height range, she just jackknifed forward from the waist, targeting nose or chin with her forehead. For taller adversaries, her move varied slightly. She would bring her arms forward and up, simply trying to get them outside her adversary's arms. The goal was not to grab or grapple; rather, she just wanted to impede their arms interfering with her next move. All in the same motion she would launch off powerful legs, her target being the underside of the chin, which she hoped to strike with her brow and the top of her forehead. She had broken a few noses and jaws over the years.

Tonight Gail had worked late. Jean Brown had night duty at University, and Gail swung by to see her. They ate dinner in the hospital cafeteria, where decent, inexpensive food was available. Jean went back on duty and Gail decided to cruise by Sally's Balls, just to see the place. It was 10:45 when she got there and was shocked to see two White guys emerge and set off down the block. One was very tall and fat; the other smallish, short and wiry. It had to be the Steiner boys.

Steen and Sten Steiner were losers, had been since birth. In the genetic lottery of intelligence, they both crapped out. Physically, Steen was much larger: six feet, three inches and a mound of Jell-O. His brother Sten was the opposite: five foot five, wiry and with a serious little-man complex. They were exactly ten months apart, now being twenty-two and twenty-three. Their mother had left town when they were still in diapers. Their father, Heinrich, was a petty criminal and drug user, in and out of jail their whole lives. They lived for a time with Heinrich's father, who was a member of the American Nazi party. He was also a drunk, who abused the boys with beatings and mental abuse, while their grandmother Helma turned a blind eye. They hated her for it and were misogynists by their teen years. They were in a number of foster homes, none good. Both had lengthy juvenile records, which were sealed. They were a product of a violent, vile world, and they were formed in its likeness. They hated women, Jews, Blacks, and immigrants. As adults they worked odd jobs, dealt a few drugs, and stole anything they could to make a buck.

They had some jewelry to hock and had slipped over to Sally's under cover of night. They knew NOPD was looking for them, but they needed the money. They had no choice, so they took a chance and walked to Sally's. The cheap fuck was sitting on a stool with his leg in an immobilizer. He gave them only fifty dollars for a Rolex watch, a diamond ring, and some other odds and ends they'd recently taken in several burglaries. They were looking for cop cars but took no notice of the Black woman driving by in a silver Kia. Gail was sure it was them, and she wanted a shot at them. She circled the block and caught up with them on a long stretch as they strolled along. She passed them and went up a full block, figuring they were headed for the Quarter. She parked and waited in the shadow for them to approach. She wore dark pants and top, and she was Black as coal. She knew they would not see her until they were on top of her. Sure enough, she heard them talking as they got closer. When she deemed the timing was right, she stepped out into their path. They stopped short, looking her over. Gail said in a firm voice, "Boys, I'd like a word." She had her gun in her right hand and held it slightly behind her.

"Nigger bitch, we gon' fuck you up," the short one hissed, taking a step forward. It was a mistake. He was now in Gail's space, and she slammed her upper body forward, catching him flush on the nose. Blood flew all over her, and he dropped like he'd been shot. Steen, the big one, was frozen. Gail raised her gun, but it was unnecessary. Steen was a follower, and he gave up without incident. Gail cuffed him and flex-cuffed Sten, who was out cold, bleeding from the nose. Backup was there in minutes, and the Steiner boys went to jail.

A day later the Steiners copped to the rapes. They denied the cinder block homicide, but in time their lawyer worked out a plea deal that sent them away for twenty to life, with the possibility of parole only after the full twenty years were served. Decker and Gail moved on. The inquiry into the reason the Steiners had been hanging around Loyola was moot and soon forgotten.

Forty-five

It had been two months since the Steiner brothers' arrest. Decker continued to work his cases. He made calls, spoke to many, and made little progress on either the death of Alisha Bondurant or the temple massacre. That was what the media had labeled the Chabad-Lubavitch attack. The mayor of New Orleans was screaming his head off, and everyone associated with the case on the law enforcement side was frustrated. It seemed the shooters had gone to ground. No other attacks occurred, but there was hysteria in the Jewish community. National media daily proclaimed the NOPD inept and the FBI a confederacy of fools. Fox News blamed antifa, with no basis whatsoever. The case was cold, and no one really had any ideas where to turn next. No chatter in the extremist community offered a clue, although the far right took the opportunity to claim if the temple had armed guards with assault rifles the massacre would not have occurred.

Gail had not spoken to Lucille Greene in quite some time. She was a bit surprised to hear from Lucille, who left a voicemail saying she had some information. Gail called her back, and she asked Gail to join her for lunch in the Loyola cafeteria at 1:00 p.m.

Gail arrived on time and found Lucille waiting for her at the entrance. They exchanged a hug and went through the line. Lucille led Gail to a table far removed from students and anyone who might overhear. After a minute or two of catching up, Gail asked, "Lucille, why did you call me? We caught those creeps, and they won't be troubling anyone for the next twenty years, assuming they live that long."

Lucille took a bite of chicken salad, nodded, and swallowed. She replied, "I know that. Read about it and saw it on the news. Remember you asked why those skinheads might be hanging around here?"

"Yes, I remember. But Lucille, it doesn't matter now. They're gone."

Lucille nodded, then spoke. "True, yes. I started asking around when you asked me to. I have many friends here on campus. I hit everyone I could think of, and nobody seemed to have a clue. Then a day or so ago the maintenance man who works in the building where the history department is stopped me. He and I had talked about the skinheads and all that. Anyhow, he stops me and tells me that he thinks one of the ladies in administration has been holding some kind of meetings in a classroom in the history department. Word of mouth only. Nothing on the boards. He doesn't believe the history department is even aware she is doing this. Here's the thing: He thinks she is holding open discussion on problems with Jews, Blacks, and anybody who can't trace their ancestry back to the Mayflower."

Gail listened intently, thinking. "You saying what I think you're saying ... Nazi stuff?"

"He thinks so. Now, he is Black as you and me, so he was not invited, understand?"

Gail said, "Yeah, I got it. What is this woman's name? What does she do here?"

Lucille pulled a small slip of paper from her purse and handed it to Gail. It read, "Penelope Thomas, office of the registrar." Gail took the paper and thanked Lucille. Gail said, "Lucille, keep this to yourself. Just let it alone. I'll take it from here. If those asshole Steiner boys were coming over for that type stuff ... well, let's just say there are some real dangerous folks in the skinhead crowd. I don't want you or June anywhere near this."

"Don't worry about that. We'll stay as far away as we can. I hope this helps some," Lucille responded. They rose, hugged again, and Gail headed for the station. She wanted to check this Penelope Thomas out, think about it a bit. There was something there, she felt it. She did not want to rush in and sound the alarm. Gail went into stealth mode.

Forty-six

ail returned to her station and sat down at her computer. She entered "Penelope Thomas" and ran a search of NOPD records. Nothing showed up; she had expected as much. Working at Loyola in administration likely meant she was not a criminal with a record. That would have been flagged, and she would have been fired or never hired in the first place. Gail next looked for her on Facebook and found a smiling woman who looked to be early forties. A quick look once again showed nothing remarkable. Gail sat back thinking about what she had, if anything, and how she might use it. After turning it over and looking from all angles, she decided her best move was to trade. She called Decker O'Day and asked him to stop by when he could. Decker suggested coffee in the morning, and they settled on The Rook Café on Freret Street.

Decker found Gail already drinking coffee and eating a pastry when he arrived. He got a medium black coffee and joined her. Decker once again congratulated Gail on the Steiner arrest. Gail's response was pure. "Someone has to keep the streets clean; otherwise we'd all be stepping in crap all day long. Listen, Decker, you still working the temple massacre, right?"

Decker perked up a bit, saying, "Yeah, for sure. We need a break, bad. The press is killing us. I hear it every day from on high. You know something?"

"Maybe," Gail said. "I need a favor in return."

"Okay, Gail, tell me what you got. If I can I'll help you even if it leads nowhere. Deal?"

Gail smiled, saying, "Deal. Remember when we met? I was looking for rapists, and you were looking for the perps in the North Claiborne killing. You got info said the mooks were skinheads. Turned out we were after the same two assholes, right?"

"Yeah, for sure. You gonna eat that whole pastry?" Decker asked, grinning.

"Damn right, for that price. Get your own. I'll still be here," Gail shot back. Decker got a couple of pastries and put them in the middle of the table on a napkin. He took one, and Gail continued. "So, at the time I could not figure out why those creeps were hitting around Loyola. You had no idea either. We busted 'em, and the question became moot. Yesterday I was at Loyola and met with Lucille Greene, a music teacher there. She'd been asking around the U about skinhead types and finally got a hit."

Decker now sat bolt upright, saying, "If this is good, you can have that other pastry."

Gail snatched the pastry and smiled. "So, turns out one of the maintenance guys who works in the building housing the history department told her about some off-radar meetings. He says he thinks this lady named Penelope Thomas is holding neo-Nazi meetings in a classroom on the quiet."

Decker nodded, thinking. "Hmmm," he said. "Go on."

"Well, so far I have nothing on this Thomas woman. She works in the registrar's office. No criminal record that I can find, looked at Facebook ... clean. When I called the maintenance guy he says he stumbled onto this thing. Left some papers in the building and went back one Saturday night about 9:30. Don't ask me why, but that's his story. Anyways, he goes in and is surprised to hear some noise from the second floor. He's thinking burglary, so he creeps up stairs and all the lights are off except for one classroom which is lit up. No windows to the outside, so not visible from outside the building. He listens, thinking he needs to go down and call the cops. What he hears shocks the hell out of him. It's all Nazi stuff—hate the niggers and Jews, conspiracy junk, all kinds of shit. He realizes this ain't no burglary, so he sneaks back down, finds a hidey-hole, and waits for them to leave. Only one he recognizes is this Thomas woman. Knew he'd seen her around. He does a bit of digging, gets her name and job description, and tells Lucille."

"Wow. Now that is interesting. So you're thinking the Steiner brothers were maybe going to these meetings, getting juiced up on propaganda?

"You got it. Makes sense. He says there are no flyers posted, no notices that he sees around, nothing. Got to be word of mouth; how else would anyone know? Why keep it so secretive if it's legitimate debate or discussion? Made the hair on the back of my neck rise, ya know?" Gail said.

"Damn right. That has a bad look. No way Loyola is approving something like that. Otherwise it would be out in the open. I'm thinking where there's smoke ..."

"Uh-huh. We thinking the same thing. Now, here's my ask. You remember the Black girl found dead last year on Tulane Avenue? Naked, dumped, cocaine and Rohypnol in her system?" Gail asked.

"Yeah, I sorta remember something like that. Nothing ever came of it, or I missed it," Decker replied.

Now Gail nodded. "Just another dead Black girl, died of a drug overdose. No suspects, not much coverage. Soon forgotten."

Decker could hear the anger in Gail's voice, saying, "Okay, yeah, help me out. Your connection?"

Gail wiped at her eyes with a napkin, saying, "I practically raised that girl. Me 'n' her Mama, Jean Brown. We grew up together in the projects, the Calliope. We fought like hell to get out, and we did. Jean's a nurse at University Hospital. Her daughter, Anita Brown, was the dead girl. Jean and I live together. We're a couple. It's damn near killed both of us. I've tried to do it off the books, but I'm a Black female working sex crimes. I got no access, no inroads, and nowhere to go with this thing. Jean, the mama, thinks a guy named Darren Nakot did it. She's got no evidence, but Nakot is Dr. Kip Nakot's son. The doctor is a neurologist at University and a really fine guy. The son is tall, handsome, and sells pharmaceuticals for some big pharma company. Has women coming and going, a real ladies' man. This guy is smart, slick, and out of my reach. I'm hoping you can use some connections to help me make some headway."

"Does this Darren dude have a record? Any priors?" Decker inquired.

"Nothing. Clean as a new Pamper. But I was in the narcotics division one day, and I heard two guys mention his name as they went down the hall. I asked a buddy to listen up, but he says all they'll say is this motherfucker is too smart to get caught. They think maybe he's a player, but they don't have a thing on him. See my problem?"

"Yeah, it sounds like my Carnival Queen case. I feel something, but I got nothing. Okay, Gail, I got to roll. I'll bring this Nazi thing to the brass, and we'll figure out what to do from there. On your case, I'll see what I can find. If I turn up anything I'll call. I'm getting a tingle on the Nazi thing; maybe my spider sense. Thanks a lot. And you're welcome for the pastry," he said, smiling. Gail threw a napkin at him, and they went to work.

Forty-seven

Jenna had waited patiently, at least in her mind, for an anchor position on the WWL morning news. She knew primetime at night was a bit of a stretch given her total lack of experience. She'd been a good scout, going to LA and bringing back tips she picked up. Yet she still had no anchor slot, and that was not right. She knew in her heart she was better than the current girl. That damn Sue Hunter was from somewhere in California, for Christ's sake. She did not sound like New Orleans, not at all. Jenna was a native, born to New Orleans royalty. She had mentioned her ability several times around the station, but nothing happened. She was entitled; the usurper was an obstacle. Not to mention Win Bentley. Despite fucking his brains out, he did not seem to be falling under Jenna's spell. He dug the sex; that much was clear. But her sense was that it was just sex, no other interest. Totally unfair to a girl with her birthright. She was in a funk and knew it.

It was now early fall, Alisha's death a memory for Jenna. She hardly gave it a thought; dead and gone; too bad, so sad. She decided maybe she could help her chances with the anchor position. Suppose something happened to Sue Hunter? Suppose she just disappeared one night, sort of like that girl from Minnesota. What was her name? Hooey, Hoosie … some weird name, didn't matter. Happened before Jenna was born, but she knew of the case: just gone one night and not a trace since. That could happen here. But how? She had to be clever. She always was; no connection to Jenna, that was her golden rule. Jenna spent several days mulling on how to carry out her mission. As with Alisha Bondurant, she had a target that must be eliminated. She had a plan for killing Sue Hunter, that part was easy. But she wanted body disposal: gone, as in never seen again.

Eventually she decided dumping the body in water would work best. She knew every bayou in the area would have gators and other meat eaters in the food chain. She studied maps on the computer at the library branch near her house. Finally, she found something she liked. The Pointe a La Hache ferry in Plaquemines Parish was closed by the state due to disrepair. It was rusting and unsafe. That community was about fifty miles from New Orleans. It was small, quiet, with not much going on. She thought it was a good site to dump a body. To test it out, Jenna drove to the deserted ferry landing one Friday night. She got there at midnight and sat until 4:30 a.m., watching. Not a soul came by, and it was quite peaceful so close to the water. It would do nicely.

She knew Dare had several pistols. She did not think he would notice one missing, at least for a few days. One Thursday night she stole the smallest one in the wee hours. Dare was fast asleep, and with her penlight she made sure it was loaded, then slipped it into her purse. She left early that Friday morning before he was awake. She went to work as usual and watched Sue Hunter do the morning news. The bitch had the audacity to ask Jenna to fetch her coffee. She gritted her teeth and did. She then asked innocently if Sue had plans for the evening. Sue did not, declaring that she was tired and planned to spend the evening at home alone. Perfect, Jenna thought. She had bought a burner phone several months earlier. That night she activated it. At 8:00 p.m. she called Sue Hunter's cell phone. Hunter picked up, and Jenna spoke through a handkerchief, disguising her voice as best she could. She was near a major road so road noise masked her voice as well. Breathlessly, she claimed to have information on those behind the temple massacre. She offered to share it with Hunter if Hunter would meet her that night. She feigned fear and said she was on the run. Hunter was wary, but the story was too big to pass up. Hunter agreed to meet the mystery caller at eleven o'clock at St. Louis Cemetery Number Two just off North Claiborne. The caller said come alone; drive roughly fifty yards into the cemetery and park. If the caller saw anyone else, the caller would not show. Hunter agreed to the terms.

Jenna got there early and parked her car deeper into the cemetery. She was dressed in Black and had the gun in her pocket. If anyone approached her she would shoot them and leave. At 11:05 Jenna, who was hiding close by, saw a car pull to a stop and cut its lights. She watched for movement for five more minutes. Seeing none, she pulled her ball cap down low and approached the passenger door. She came up from behind and kept her face above the roofline, tapping on the window. Hunter startled but, seeing a female profile, popped the locks. Jenna swung inside, gun in hand. Hunter's face registered surprise at the gun coming up and the sight of Jenna's face. Before she could utter a word Jenna shot her twice in the chest, pop, pop. The gun was a .25 caliber and made little noise. Jenna ran around the car and dragged the woman out of the car into the grass. She retrieved a vinyl tarp she had hidden close by and rolled Hunter up in it. She wrapped the ends with duct tape to stop leakage as best she could. She then dragged the body to the trunk of Hunter's car. She struggled to hoist it in; damn heavy, that's what a dead body was. Start to finish it was twenty minutes' work. She hopped in the driver's seat and set off for Highway 39 to Pointe a La Hache.

The drive took about an hour. Jenna drove a couple miles under the speed limit. She arrived around 12:30 a.m. and cruised the ferry landing. All quiet, nobody in sight. She pulled in as far as she dared and hopped out. She wanted to work quickly and did so. It was hard work, and she struggled dragging the body out onto the landing. Reaching the end, she pulled a folding knife from her pocket. She unrolled the tarp until she could see the torso. She stripped the woman's clothing and without hesitation, plunged the knife into the woman's abdomen. No floaters, not on Jenna's watch. She cut a long deep incision in the torso and then did some work on the legs to make sure. Satisfied, she rolled the body off the end of the abandoned ferry. It sank, and she then flung the burner phone and knife as far out as she could. She dipped the bloody tarp in to wash off the blood, rolled it up and took it back to the car. She put the clothing in a trash bag she had brought and set off toward New Orleans. It was now ten minutes until two in the morning. Jenna tossed the dead woman's clothes out along the side of the road. She waited a couple miles per item, and soon they were gone. She drove back to North Claiborne and parked on the side of the road close to the cemetery entrance. It was now 3:07, and the street was deserted. She left the keys in the ignition and racked the seat back so it would look as if a taller male had driven the car. She had on thin latex gloves and had left no prints. She grabbed the tarp and hiked off to her car. She was gone within minutes. She figured someone would steal the car. If not, what would the police find? An abandoned car and some blood spatter? No big deal and no connection to Jenna. She'd worn a hair net and been extra careful not to leave DNA. She stuffed the tarp down a storm sewer on a side street on her way home. It was somewhere close to 4:00 a.m. when she let herself into her house. Exhausted, she put her clothes and shoes in the washer and turned it on. She would throw them away later when she woke up. She planned to return Dare's gun as soon as she had an opportunity. She slept like a baby.

Forty-eight

ecker asked for and got a meeting with Captain Winston and Bill Kearney a couple hours after meeting with Gail. He had taken a look at Penelope Thomas on Facebook and tried the same records check as Gail, just to be thorough. He found nothing but was not discouraged in the least. He met with Winston and Kearney at 11:00 that Friday morning. They sat in Kearney's temporary office at Tulane PD. Each took coffee, and Winston asked Decker to take the lead.

"I met this morning with a detective from our sex crimes unit. She works out of the Broad Street Station. She and I were after the same two assholes a couple months ago, the Steiner brothers. She made the collar. Turned out those two were good for a couple rapes near Loyola and had dropped a cinder block off an overpass, killing a Black lady on North Claiborne. We wondered why two skinheads were hanging around Loyola. They had tried to grab a fourteen-year-old girl on Loyola's campus a few days before Gail rolled 'em up. Girl's mother teaches music there. When they were in custody, the question dropped; didn't matter what drew 'em to Loyola. We both forgot about it. Then a couple days ago this maintenance guy stops the girl's mom on campus and tells her about some unusual activity he stumbled across. Seems he discovered that a woman in the registrar's office is mixed up with secret meetings involving Nazi types."

Winston broke in, "Nazi types? At Loyola? That crowd is as Catholic as the Pope. Is this real, Decker? Sounds a bit out there to me."

Bill Kearney jumped in. "No, Captain, actually it does not surprise me. Let me give you guys a glimpse into what I see pretty routinely these days. White nationalism is a big thing in this country currently. Hate crimes have increased; anti-Semitism is on the rise and has been for a while. I'm not saying all the White nationalists are Nazis; nothing like that. I am saying the neo-Nazis, of which there are far more than you might imagine, need the Jews as their punching bag. Hatred of Jews is at the core of the Nazi beliefs. Many White nationalists subscribe, at least in part, to all the conspiracy stuff. The Nazis use the Jews as a sort of malleable enemy. They are either superpowerful, controlling the world through banking and politics, or they are a weak, inferior race polluting the bloodlines and promoting the undesirables: Blacks, Browns, you name it. Those notions seem contradictory if you really think about it, but reality has nothing to do with what the Nazis are after. Their goal is to win hearts and minds, so they don't care which version you believe as long as you believe one of them."

"Okay, I can see that," Winston replied. "What does that have to do with Loyola and this lady?"

Kearney continued, "Captain, it is not unusual to see anti-Semitism in academic settings. We've found Nazis in academia, professions like medicine or law, just about everywhere. These folks are motivated by a variety of things. Some by ideologies they may have, others by personal grudges they may hold for any number of reasons. It may be the environment they were raised in, some incident in their life, or just the need for a scapegoat to blame for what troubles them. Whatever it is that motivates them really does not matter. The important thing to understand is that they use their beliefs to justify violence. We saw anti-government ideology in the Oklahoma City bombing. Something radicalizes these folks to become extremists. When they do, they can become quite dangerous. It's not unusual to find anti-Semites in the military, law enforcement, or in ordinary people. What I'm trying to say is that Loyola University is likely against anti-Semitism, but there may be those few who work there who hate Jews."

Winston nodded his head yes, saying, "That makes a lot more sense. I just could not get my head around Loyola being against Jews on a policy level. Too many good people over there. Hell, I'm friends with some of 'em. So, Bill, this is outside my area of expertise. What do you think our next moves should be, assuming you think it's worth a look?"

Bill Kearney spoke authoritatively. "Damn right it's worth a look. It's the first sniff we've gotten since the EL thing. We're nowhere on that, and I don't have to tell you we're being crucified daily by the national media. Decker, this is good stuff. Definitely worth a look. Here's what I propose. Captain, your guys need to keep this woman under surveil-lance. Surreptitiously, mind you, we don't want her to know we are looking at all. I'll leave that to you. I have some folks in the bureau who do nothing but research. I'll put them on a deep dive into who she is, what her story is. Understand, guys, this may take a while. It may be a rabbit hole, but it's something at a time when we have nothing. These types are paranoid, and if they are in and around academia, they're likely bright. They may be warped in their views, but that does not mean they are not intelligent. Decker, keep doing what you've been doing. Leave this angle alone for now. We'll do the research, and Captain Winston can put some undercover guys to work. Agreed?"

Winston and Decker both voiced a yes. They walked out together, and Winston patted Decker on the back. "Good work. I had no idea."

Decker responded, "Neither did I. Captain, Gail deserves some real credit here. Without her, we'd have none of this. She asked if I could look into a death ... her friend's daughter. Found dead of a drug overdose, nude and dumped on Tulane

Avenue a year or so ago. Can I use you to cover my six on this if I catch some flak? I'll work it in with my Carnival Queen inquiry, it won't affect my performance." Winston agreed, and Decker headed for his desk.

Forty-nine

Over the weekend Decker relaxed a bit. It was the first time in several months that he had not spent part of the weekend working. He had gotten nothing more on the Alisha Bondurant case. He could find no way to put Jenna Dupreaux in the picture for Alisha's death, although he had a nagging feeling about Jenna. He thought the pigtails were over the top; it struck him as manipulative and a put-on to make her appear young and innocent. Jenna was a piece of work, that was for sure. He knew she was smart, had money, and was a planner. Whether she was a killer was another matter; he had nothing concrete. Her lie about weed made him suspicious. There was also the other stuff Aline Bondurant had shared. All in all, he had his suspicions. But cases were not made on suspicions, so he let it go and enjoyed the down time.

Captain Winston put Penelope Thomas under twenty-four-hour surveillance. The chief approved it, desperate for a break in the temple massacre. Bill Kearney had his diggers going full tilt. He had agents quietly speak with people who knew Thomas when she was growing up. They did background workups. One thing popped when he got an email from a researcher on Sunday morning. The email said that when Penelope was twelve her parents divorced. They were Catholics, which piqued his interest. Even more interesting was that two years later Penelope's father married a Jewish woman and converted to Judaism. That sent a charge through Bill Kearney; he felt a slight tremor. The kind of tremor he got when he thought important information on one of his cases had come to light. In itself, nothing; in the context of secretive Nazi gatherings and the temple massacre, it reso-nated. He immediately made some calls and put agents in the field to work trying to quietly get a picture of how Penelope Thomas reacted to those events years ago. His sense was that this was a significant nugget of information and that they were on to something.

Monday morning rolled around, and Decker reported to Tulane PD to start his week. Sometime that morning he overheard some chatter about a missing news anchor. He was only half listening until he heard WWL mentioned, the local TV station affiliated with CBS. He jumped up and hurried over to the Tulane cops who were drinking coffee and chatting. Decker interrupted, "I couldn't help but over-hear your conversation. What's this about a missing news anchor?"

The lady officer replied, "Yeah, it's a developing story. Sue Hunter, morning news anchor at WWL, did not show for work. That got the folks at the station wondering. Calls to her cell went straight to voicemail. Seems no one has seen her since Friday. They don't know much, but it's got every-body worried."

Decker thought, "Oh, shit," but said only, "Thanks. Sorry for the interruption." He went straight to the break room where a TV was tuned in to catch local news. Sure enough, the media were in full frenzy over one of their own gone missing. No one seemed to have any real facts, but Decker had a sinking feeling in the pit of his stomach. He headed for his car and WWL.

Fifty

Decker got to the North Rampart Street location at noon. He parked and went inside. He spotted a couple of uniformed cops and beelined over to them. He flashed his shield, saying, "Hey, guys. I'm Detective O'Day. What's going on with the Hunter woman?"

The officer whose name tag read Spain responded, "We don't know yet. We got a call this morning to do a welfare check on a Sue Hunter. Called in by the station manager, the lady over there in the blue dress. We go to the address, knock on the door, and get no answer. We call the manager, Ms. Crowley, and report the no answer to our knock. She says look for her car, it's a white Toyota Camry. We look around the lot—she lives in Ten Oaks apartments out Magazine Street. Don't see a white Camry. We go ask the apartment manager to let us in, and he does. Place is clean, neat. No signs of a disturbance but no cell phone and no purse. Bed is made, everything looks normal. Like she just went out and never came back. From there we drove around the area for an hour or so looking and our sarge sent us over here to talk to these folks. That's what we got so far. Are you in charge, sir?

"No, I'm not. I got wind of this and came on my own. I ah ... I have another case, and this caught my attention. Thanks guys, sounds like you did a good job."

The other cop, a woman named Ramon, said, "Crowley told us the Hunter woman is very conscientious. Says she's never late, works hard. No drugs or alcohol issues. Doesn't think this girl has a steady boyfriend or anything. Kinda spooky, you ask me."

Decker nodded, saying, "Yeah, kinda spooky sounds right to me. I'm going over to talk with Ms. Crowley." He walked over and introduced himself to the manager, who told him her name was Amy Crowley. She was White, somewhere in her fifties, with a concerned look on her face. She told Decker much the same story as the uniforms had and expressed real concern that something was wrong.

She said, "Detective, Sue is a gem. She works like a Trojan. For her to just disappear like this ... no calls, cell goes straight to messages. I just know something has happened. She's either hurt or something bad has happened to her. I've got staff calling the hospitals. Have you been assigned to this ... case?"

"No," Decker said, just as Jenna Dupreaux stepped out of an office across the studio. Jenna headed his way. Decker thought to reach in his pocket and grab his cell phone. He turned slightly to shield her view, hitting record and putting it back in the inner pocket of his sport coat. Jenna marched up big as life and grabbed his arm.

"Decker, I'm so glad you're here. We're frantic; worried sick about Sue," Jenna said, concern dripping from her voice. "I mean, she and I spent a good bit of time together here at the station. Just last Friday I walked down to Twelfth Night and brought her coffee. Do you think something has happened to her? I'm frightened. Are we in danger?"

"No, I don't think you're in any danger," Decker replied.

"Are you on this ... disappearance? I thought you worked homicide?" Jenna asked.

Decker looked Jenna in the eye, saying, "No, I just heard she was missing and thought you might know something." He watched for her response, which was immediate.

Jenna looked shocked, taking a half step back. "Me? Why would I know something? I mean, I just work here. We didn't socialize or anything. Not the same circles at all. I don't even know where Sue lived." Decker heard the word "lived" and thought, "Goddamn it," although his expression remained unchanged.

Decker said, "Okay, Jenna. I've got to go. Be seeing you around."

Jenna watched him walk away. She followed him to the door and looked out as he got in his car and pulled into the street. Her mind was racing. She wondered what he knew.

Fifty-one

As the week went along, the noise surrounding Sue Hunter's disappearance grew louder. The media peered into the past and made comparisons to the Jodi Huisentruit disappearance in Mason City, Iowa, back in the 90s. There were claims of a secret lover, sightings as far away as Delaware, and a lot of noise with no real meat on the bone. The cops had not found her car, which seemed to have vanished off the earth. The cops were puzzled, unsure exactly what they were dealing with. In time they got Hunter's cell phone records, but that led to a call on Friday night from a phone that was no longer in service and had no owner attached—a burner. Decker, for his part, shared his concerns with his lieutenant, who passed them along to Captain Crunch. Word came back down that Decker had plenty on his plate—Alisha Bondurant and the temple massacre. Those were his priorities, and he was not to go pushing a rich, White debutante on the strength of his Irish gut. Captain Crunch's exact words, quoted to Decker verbatim from Double L, were "Tell that Paddy dude I'm gon' put a foot in his White ass, he keep's messin' with things outside his lane."

For his part, Decker knew what he knew. But knowing and proving were very different things. He did have plenty to do. He had learned from Captain Winston that the FBI had interviewed people who said Penelope Thomas hated Jewish people after her father remarried and converted. Background revealed that Penelope's mother was an alcoholic and promiscuous, but none of that seemed to matter to Penelope. She was a good worker, having been at the registrar's office for the last sixteen years. She was quiet and kept her opinions to herself for the most part. But there was little doubt she had a virulent hatred of Jewish people. Surveillance revealed that she spent time in the company of a history professor at Loyola. His name was Frank Gross, and he had tenure, being forty-seven with twenty-five years at the university. He taught a variety of courses, was well-liked, and had a spotless record. The watchers believed the two were intimate based on comings and goings but had seen nothing out of the ordinary. No secret meetings, no skin-heads or thuggish types about. Just a couple of middle-aged folks living normal lives. Kearney was unmoved, saying give it time. He knew they were in the long game unless they caught a lucky break.

Decker continued to do interviews with the wealthy and connected in New Orleans. He was interested in Roe Stilton, in addition to the death of Alisha Bondurant. He ran into an old law school friend one day in a sandwich shop, and they sat down to catch up. The friend, Jonathon Ball, worked at one of the large downtown law firms. He had been a partner for several years and his father had been a lawyer too prior to his death. As they talked and chatted about various things, Decker thought to ask Ball about Roe Stilton. Ball swallowed and said, "I don't know the man. I know of him, though. My father swore he was a crook. You know my dad died at sixty-two. His heart gave out. He litigated like his hair was on fire. He said Roe Stilton was a dishonest and unethical little shit. I don't know details, but Dad felt like he was always on the fringes with just enough deniability to keep out of the fire. He hated the man. said he was racist to the bone and a 'goddamned Nazi.' Why he thought so I cannot tell you, but make no mistake, Roe Stilton was on his shit list. Why are you interested in Stilton? I doubt he's committed any homicides."

Decker was most interested but did not want to do or say anything that might lead his friend Jonathon to start any rumors. He knew that the courthouse rumor mill was rife with gossip on all things. He did not want to alert Stilton that someone might be looking at him. He quickly said, "I'm really more interested in Crawford, his son. He seems to be into drugs, and the drug scene is another dimension. I don't think Crawford has done anything, but I kinda had the idea he might know someone connected to a case I had. It's all over now. I met the old man once and was more curious than anything else. Pretty pompous little guy."

Jonathon reacted, "That is an understatement based on what Dad said. He said Stilton thought he was superior. His family was from Germany somewhere back in the day, and they changed their name to Stilton at some point. At least that's what dad said. I don't know; it might not be true. Dad could get a hard-on for someone, it was his nature. Pure bulldog; killed him in the end. Oh, well, I gotta get back to the office. Great seeing you, Decker. Be well. I've got the tab. Business development for the firm, ya know?" Decker smiled and thanked him, thinking one just never knows where useful information might come from. He had a smile on his face as he headed for the Mustang.

Fifty-two

Decker decided he would take a page from the FBI playbook and do a bit of surveillance on Jenna Dupreaux. He did not know what else to do; nothing was moving. The Thomas woman was going about her business, and so far there was nothing to see. The agents had spoken to the maintenance man, Clarence Coleman, who confirmed all that Gail had learned. He knew who Professor Gross was and said he had not been in the meeting he stumbled upon; or at least he had not seen Gross leaving. It was possible Gross had come and gone earlier or went out another door. Either way the only connection to the professor at that point was the nocturnal visits of Penelope Thomas. She visited Gross at his home a couple of nights a week. There was still no sign of Sue Hunter, and her car had not turned up. The cops had no way of knowing, but Jenna's plan worked to perfection. A druggie wandered up on Hunter's car. He was looking to break a window and steal something for drug money. He was shocked to find the doors open and the keys in the ignition. He got in, saw the blood spatter, and drove straight to a no-questions-asked chop shop. He now had drug money for a week, and the car was gone for good.

Decker set up on Jenna's place just after dark on Tuesday night. He watched until 11:00, when her lights went out. Wednesday was a repeat, so on Thursday he picked her up as she left work. He followed her as she picked up her laundry and then went grocery shopping. She went home, but at five minutes to eight she backed out of her garage and set off. He followed her to the Charlotte Commons Condominiums in the Garden District. He stayed well back, but from a distance he thought she must have had a key. She walked up to the door and went inside immediately. He sat for the next four hours and finally decided she was staying the night. He made a note of the unit number and went home to bed. The next morning he checked and learned that Darren Nakot was the unit owner. A bit of backgrounding showed that he was thirty-one and the son of Dr. Nakot, a neurologist at University Hospital. He worked for a pharmaceuticals company and had a clean record. No arrests, no traffic violations, and nothing that stood out. Suddenly he recalled his conversation with Gail, and it all came back; son of a bitch, he thought. Darren Nakot was the guy Gail's friend suspected in the death of Anita Brown. Decker did not know what to make of it, but he was keenly interested. He called Gail and asked if the name Jenna Dupreaux meant anything to her. Gail did not know the name, and Decker filled her in on who Jenna was and why he had an interest.

Gail listened to the story and then said, "Damn, Decker, that's a lot to swallow. You really think this White society gal is runnin' around killing folks? That don't seem right. Not sayin' you're wrong, but she ain't the usual type out whackin' folks, you know?"

"You are right about one thing, she is not the usual type. I think she has a screw loose. Some incidents along the way suggest she may be a psychopath. I don't know a lot about those kind of folks, but I know enough to know they can be dangerous. I asked one of the department psychologists who helps with interrogations sometimes. She told me psychopathy is defined by certain character traits. She boiled it down to the fact that psychopaths often feel entitled to whatever it is they want. Some of them, the rarer ones, will kill to fulfill their desires. Lots of psychology in there. This girl is very smart and very manipulative. She met me one day for a drink wearing pigtails and trying to look like a sixteen-year-old schoolgirl."

Gail laughed out loud at that one, saying, "Only a White girl. Holy shiitakes, man, that is some serious mind games. She was tryin' to mindfuck you."

Now Decker laughed, saying, "She might have been ready to fuck more than my mind. I got the vibe that she wanted to know if I was interested. She's spending nights over at Darren Nakot's place. You know that name."

"You serious? Now that is interesting. Pharmaceutical sales, Anita dead by drugs, your Carnival Queen dead by drugs. Makes my cynical mind wonder. You feel me?"

"Oh, yeah, I feel you. It's a new connection, and I'm getting a warning vibe. I think you are too!"

"Damn right I am. I'll hang back. No way that White girl misses my Black behind if I start sniffin' around her. You got reason and authority. I'm more excited than I've been in a long time. I'm sure glad you decided to sit on her a bit. I'll talk to Jean, give her the news, and ask her to listen up for anything on this society girl. Spell that last name for me, please." Decker did, and the call ended. He felt a tingle.

Fifty-three

Professor Frank Gross lay naked and sweating on the bed. He was in the Alder Hotel on Magnolia Street. He had just finished his weekly tryst with Beth Barnett, an FBI agent in the New Orleans office. Beth was thirty-seven, unmarried, and a career girl. She had no desire for a husband, kids, diapers, and the lot. She liked sex, good food, and doing as she pleased. She and Frank shared a number of things. They both did not want commitment. They both liked their sex rough and tumble. And they were both Nazis, American Nazis, mind you, born in the US of A. They were virulent anti-Semites. Frank was enthralled with the views of Father Coughlin and Henry Ford. Ford had been anti-Semitic and made no secret of it. Coughlin was a Catholic priest whom Gross had studied. He came to believe Coughlin and Ford were correct, and that Jews were a menace on many levels. Barnett was an Ohio girl whose working-class family suffered when several factories closed. Her parents blamed the Jews. She was a child whose family fell into poverty, and she accepted her parents' views on the cause. She grew up hating Jews for that reason; she found common ground with Gross in her antipathy.

They met in a class she had audited in the evening a couple years earlier. Gross had been a panelist one evening, and she sensed that he had some reluctance to condemn all the views held by the Nazi party. He certainly did not come out and say so, but something told her he had some views he was reluctant to open up about. She approached him after the class ended, and they wound up getting coffee. Over time they became intimate, and as the trust grew, they shared views. Bottom line: They hated the Jews. Gross had a sort of loose alliance of those who shared that view. He was very guarded with information, especially since Barnett was in the FBI. Gross wanted proof that Beth Barnett was not a plant sent to entrap him and his associates. She agreed, within reason, and eventually a plan was developed. A Jewish banker was giving one of the Nazi sympathizers difficulty over a loan. The banker would not give approval on a project that Gross's group supported. Beth Barnett was told that there were compromising pictures of the man with a woman not his wife. She was to contact him, tell him what she had, and set up a meeting to leverage him into making the loan. All she had to do was make the phone call and set up the meeting. Someone else would meet the man and Blackmail him into cooperation.

Beth agreed and made the call from a burner phone Frank Gross gave her. Frank was with her to make sure she did it properly. Beth made the call, set the meet, and thought it was done. The next day she learned the banker was dead, shot to death. Frank then played a recording he had made on his cell phone of Beth's call. He told her it was a raw deal, but they had to be sure. Beth was pissed at Frank on a personal level, but the death of the Jewish banker did not seem to trouble her. She was in deep and okay with it provided Frank assured her he had the only copy of the recording. He did, and they moved forward.

A couple of years went by, and Beth was aware of the coming attack on Temple Chabad-Lubavitch. Her sole responsibility was to be an inside ear on FBI progress. For several months there was nothing. She knew of the EL information, but that led nowhere. Then she learned that a woman named Penelope Thomas was under surveillance and had been visiting a Professor Frank Gross a couple of nights a week. Beth did not care about Frank's sex life outside of their trysts. She was greatly concerned about the FBI taking an interest in Frank himself. As long as the FBI's eyes were focused on the Thomas woman, all was well. She knew nothing of the attack and merely held some meaningless meetings where skinheads and bigots came to share hatred of Jews and Blacks. But if things changed, she would have to act in self-preservation.

Fifty-four

Decker had asked Bill Kearney to put his diggers on Roe Stilton. When Kearney asked why, Decker shared the information he had gotten from his lawyer buddy. Kearney agreed, and within a couple of days he summoned Decker to his office. He began, "I heard back from my background team. It seems Mr. Stilton is quite an interesting guy. The family name used to be Stiehl. When his father came over soon after World War II he changed his name to Stilton. They dug pretty hard, and while there's nothing concrete, they think he may have been part of the Reichstag, Hitler's rubber-stamp government. Entry records show he was from a small town in Germany, but my folks think that was a forgery and that he was likely from Munich. Bottom line is they suspect he was a full-blown Nazi; whether he wore the uniform is immaterial."

"Damn. The old man was right, then. Maybe Roe Stilton is right in the channel with his heritage."

"Likely, based on my experience. I've put my best financial people looking into Stilton's finances. These type guys are very clever. The Germans are a smart people, prone to detail. If he's funding terrorism or giving to Nazi sympathizers, it will be well hidden. The man has a lot of money, I can tell you that. We think some of it is offshore. That raises other questions. Why? Is it tax evasion? Asset protection? Or is he using offshore money to fund things like the temple massacre? Those will be hard questions to answer. Turks and Caicos money is very difficult to track, and there are so many ways to hide payments that eventually fund terror. Anyway, I wanted you to know that you may be onto something. Lots of German descendants in New Orleans, so no way to say for sure at this juncture. Keep doing your job, Decker. You've turned up some good stuff. Captain Winston thinks so too."

Decker could not help himself. He smiled, replying, "Thanks. Good to hear. Sir, can I ask a big favor?"

Kearny responded, "Sure. I don't know if I can say yes, but no harm in asking. What is it?"

"This is a big ask, but I was wondering if you could send a couple of FBI guys over to knock on the door of a guy named Darren Nakot. He's a pharmaceutical sales rep, lives in the Charlotte Common Condominiums. Alls I want is for them to knock on his door and ask if he knows Jenna Dupreaux. They can ask a couple questions, then leave. I don't care what he says. I want to rattle this girl's cage. I suspect she has killed several folks and slid by so far. She's smart and devious. I need to shake her tree, see if she makes a mistake."

"You think she's a serial killer, Decker? That's rare. It's outside my patch. I tell you what. I can't send them over to inquire about information on this Dupreaux woman. But I can send them over to ask if he knows anyone who is anti-Semitic. Any skinhead/Nazi types. That fits with our investigation into the temple massacre. And in the course of the conversation I can have them ask if he knows a Jenna Dupreaux. Just drop it in without giving any reason. How's that?"

"Damn fine, is how that is. I really appreciate it, Sir."

That afternoon two FBI agents showed up at Darren Nakot's door. They later reported that Nakot was cool, calm, and collected. He knew no skinhead types and had no connections to Nazi sympathizers. He admitted to being friends with Jenna Dupreaux but did not believe she could possibly be involved in the shootings at the Chabad Temple. The discussion was brief, but the fox had been loosed in the henhouse. Now Decker sat back and waited. He had no idea what might happen, but he had stirred the pot.

Fifty-five

Roe Stilton, like all good Nazis, had trip wires in place to set off alarms if anyone came snooping about. He received an email one day that read simply, "Saw some mutual friends recently. Come visit soon. Best, William B." He had no friend named William B; it was a message to call Professor Frank Gross on a burner phone. He later got a text of nine digits, which he expected. It would be a burner Gross had activated. Stilton left his office and bought a TracFone with prepaid minutes in a little bodega in Algiers. He called Gross, who picked up immediately. Gross was in a bit of a panic. He launched in. "The FBI is on Penelope Thomas."

Stilton asked, "Who is that? I don't recognize the name."

Gross replied, "She's a friend of mine. Actually, she's more than that. We've been sleeping together weekly for some time. I'm not sure what to do or what it means. But I thought you should know."

"Can she lead them to us, to the Chabad thing?" Stilton inquired.

"No, no, of course not. She knows nothing of that. She holds meetings every couple months in the history department. Usually on a Saturday night, word of mouth only. Gets skinhead types and sympathizers to our cause. Occasionally someone who is useful turns up. But mostly she just does propaganda against Jews, Blacks, the lot of them. Stirs anger, keeps things on the boil. That sort of thing. But I'm worried she'll lead them to me eventually. I can't just punt her. She'll go ballistic. I don't know what to do."

Roe Stilton knew what to do. He replied, "Okay, Frank. Calm yourself. We're buried deep here. Just sit tight and let me think about it a bit. I'll talk with the council and see what the thinking is. For now, act normal and keep seeing her. Nothing out of the ordinary. Got it?"

"Yes, I've got it. But move it along. I feel exposed."

Stilton assured Gross that all would be well. He said, "I'll get back to you. May be a day or so. Just act normal, for Christ's sake."

As soon as Gross rang off, Stilton made a call to J. R. Pine. He said, "You still soaking up the sun?"

"Gettin' laid a lot. Still here. Why?"

"Another job. I need some houses painted. I'll text you the addresses. You up for it?" Stilton asked

"Work is work. Somebody's gotta do it. Usual terms for a house?" Pine asked.

"Yes, the usual. Nothing special about these houses. Let me know when they're done."

"No problem, chief. We'll git 'er done," Pine said, hitting end on his phone.

Fifty-six

Jenna got a call from Dare shortly after the FBI visited him. He asked her to meet him at The Pressed Grape for a glass of wine at 7:30. He was cryptic, and Jenna knew something was up. She cleaned up and drove to The Grape, arriving a few minutes late. She saw Dare sitting at an outside table, a bit removed from everyone else. Two glasses of wine were in place; he had one, and the other was obviously for her. She made her way, leaning down to kiss his cheek. She whispered, "What's up?" and took a seat.

Dare said, "Have a sip of wine. It's your favorite." Jenna complied, nodding her appreciation. He continued, using a low voice just above a whisper. "The FBI just knocked on my door an hour ago. Some bullshit about the temple massacre and Nazis. I didn't have a clue and told them I didn't. But in the conversation they asked about you."

Jenna nearly spit her sip of wine out. She was jolted to her core, saying, "What the fuck, Dare? Me? Why would they mention me? I am not a Nazi and don't have anything to do with the temple shooting. Are you sure you heard them correctly?

"Your name is Jenna Dupreaux. That is the name the agent asked about: Jenna Dupreaux. Of course, I told them I knew you and knew you were not involved in the Chabad shooting. But they asked, and it was you they asked about. Unless there's another Jenna D here in New Orleans."

"Fucking hell," Jenna said under her breath. "It's got to be that detective, Decker. He keeps sniffing around me. Son of a bitch. But the FBI makes no sense. I know nothing about the temple thing. I didn't kill any Jews, and I didn't put anyone up to it. Christ, I don't know any Nazis or skinhead types." Jenna began to sniffle a bit. She continued, "It's so unfair. I mean, this guy blames me for everything. It's not right, you know?"

"Sure, Jenna," Dare said. "I know you did nothing wrong. I just wanted you to know, that's all. Maybe we need to stay apart for a bit. Let things cool down. Right?"

Jenna nodded, saying, "Yeah, for sure. Thanks for the heads-up. I'm going home to think. Thanks for the wine, Dare. We'll just lie low, and it'll all blow over. See ya." With that Jenna scooped her purse, gave Dare another peck on the cheek, and left. She went straight home, took a Vistaril, and put on her music. She was soon lost in thought.

Jenna's mind drifted as she considered the FBI visit and all that had happened. She continued to wonder what Decker might know. Could he possibly know about Casey Ellis? Jenna flashed back to her first year at LSU. She met Casey during rush and was instantly attracted to her. Casey was the body opposite of Jenna. She was an ectomorph, all legs and arms. She had a tiny waist, was small-breasted, and had jet black hair. She was from somewhere in Kansas, some Podunk town on the plains. They hit it off, and although they chose different sororities, they remained friends. Jenna pledged Delta Zeta, while Casey became a Kappa.

One Friday night they bumped into one another in Bengal Tap Room. Over beer and burgers, they caught up on how school was going, their social life, and more. Casey was a bit homesick, finding Baton Rouge a long way from Kansas and her plain roots. Jenna was sympathetic, and they ended up buying a six pack of beer and going to Jenna's dorm room. From there, Jenna was not sure exactly how things transpired; she was buzzed. The next thing she knew they were passionately kissing and spent the night enjoying one another. Jenna and Casey continued their secret trysts for the next several months.

As Christmas break got closer, Jenna began to get wind of talk within the DZ house that Jenna had a female friend that she was too close to. Jenna denied it, and LSU let out for the Christmas holidays. Jenna went home worried about her reputation and unsure of what course of action she should take. Suzanne noticed that Jenna was not herself, preoccupied with something. One evening Jenna came home a bit tipsy from being out with friends. Suzanne engaged her in conversation, ultimately asking, "Jenna, what is wrong, dear? You seem out of sorts. Is everything all right at school?" Jenna teared up and told her mother of her affair with Casey Ellis. Suzanne, always on the lookout for Jenna's reputation, seized control immediately.

"We'll have to do something, Jenna. This will ruin you at the DZ house, and none of the boys will want anything to do with you. Who is this, this Casey girl? Who are her people?"

Jenna, for once, was concerned for her friend. She replied, "Mother, she's just a sweet girl from Kansas. Some cow town out there, I don't know. I don't think they have money. She never dresses up, and she doesn't have a car. I don't know much else about her. But I don't want her hurt. I mean, I don't want ... Oh, I don't know what I want. I just wish she would go to another school. That would be enough; no one would mention it again if she left LSU."

Suzanne thought for a moment, then said, "All right, darling, let Mama think about it. We'll figure something out. Don't you worry; I'll fix it. Haven't I always fixed it?"

"Yes, Mother, you have. I trust you. I'm going to bed. I'm pooped." A week later, on the eve of Christmas, Suzanne told her that she had a solution. She told Jenna to keep quiet and trust her. She was sure she could arrange for the Ellis girl to transfer to another school.

Fifty-seven

Jenna did not return to LSU the spring semester of her freshman year. She traveled to Italy where she traveled extensively, enjoying the food and art. When spring semester began Casey Ellis returned to find that nude photos of her in salacious poses had been sent to every fraternity and sorority on campus. The email subject line read, "Slutty coed." The photos were graphic in nature, and Casey was summarily kicked out of the Kappa house. She could not believe what was happening. Everywhere she went she was recognized as the girl in the photos. She knew she had not posed for any photos of this type, but it made no difference. The word was out, and Casey quickly grew depressed. She tried to tell people the body was not hers, but no one seemed to care. She withdrew from school three weeks into her second semester and returned to Kansas. Her depression got worse, as the small town she was from learned of the incident. The population was only 3,729 people, and there were no secrets in such a small town.

As spring turned to summer Casey withdrew even more. She refused to go out with her friends and often did not leave the house for days. Both her parents worked and were gone most of the day. Right before the Fourth of July Casey hanged herself in the garage, tying a rope to the open rafters. Her mother found her after work. An ambulance was summoned, but Casey had been dead for several hours. Her parents were crushed. Their only child was gone, and all they knew was that she had told them the photos at LSU were not her. She had never revealed her affair with Jenna, so they had no knowledge of that story and its possible connection to her death. They were left with numbing grief and nothing more. At LSU, she was soon forgotten and only later did the Kappa house learn of her death. They viewed it as a horrible tragedy, but there was nothing for them to do other than go on with life.

Jenna returned to LSU the fall of that year, where she picked up right where she had left off. The rumors were long forgotten. She did well in school and made up the lost semester by going summer term of the following year. Jenna suspected her mother when she learned of the photos sent to the Greeks on campus. Suzanne denied any involvement and was glad to put that chapter behind her. No one was aware that Suzanne had located a sleazy photographer who was willing to photoshop Casey's head onto the body of a porn actress of similar build. It was a good job, professionally done. The emailing to the LSU fraternities and sororities was simple, and he had covered his tracks well. He sent the photos out through a site on the dark web, and tracing them was next to impossible, even if anyone had tried. Jenna was back in the catbird seat, protected by Suzanne and their money. It was a familiar place for her, and she thrived from there. She also became more aware that she had to think things through and make sure there was no blowback to her actions.

Fifty-eight

Pine and Elrod checked into a cheap motel outside New Orleans city limits. They had addresses for a woman and a man. They were pros, so they did what pros do: They set up their own surveillance on their targets. They wanted to get a good look, make sure they had the right people and learn their routines. No rushing in; that got you caught or killed. They targeted the man first, as he was the priority. They watched him for a couple of days and were sitting on his house one evening when a car pulled into his drive. To their surprise, a woman got out and went inside. They were pretty sure she was their other target. Nice, they thought, two birds with one stone. Still, they decided to watch a bit before moving. It proved to be a smart move. A couple minutes later a car pulled up down the block and cut its lights. Pine pulled his night vision monocular and looked at the dark shape where the car had parked. In green of infrared he could plainly see two men, both wearing ties. He knew immediately, saying to El, "We got company. Couple of feebs just pulled up down the block. Gotta be tailin' the tail," chuckling at his own joke.

Elrod responded, "So, how you wanna play this? We goin' in or pulling back? Your call."

Pine smiled in the dark. He said, "El, I always enjoy fucking somebody over. Let's do 'em right under the noses of these law dogs. I'm gonna pull out and head the other direction. Just another car leaving this hood. We'll park a couple blocks over, give it thirty minutes for the two inside to get naked and sweaty, then slip in and kill 'em both. We'll be gone, and the feebs won't know a damn thing. I bet they get their asses chewed tomorrow." Both men guffawed at that thought, and five minutes later Pine backed into a driveway and drove off in the opposite direction from the FBI. He went two blocks over, found a quiet spot, and pulled to the curb. It was 10:30 when they left their SUV. The dome light was switched off. They were dressed in all black; both had silenced 9-millimeter pistols, courtesy of the US government for which they had worked. They slipped through back yards and came up behind Gross's house. They went over his fence with ease and crept to his back door. Pine motioned for El to peek in the kitchen window, which he did. He hand signaled the all-clear sign. Pine pulled a lock rake from his fatigues and set to work on the lock. It was a basic residential lock, and Pine had it open in under a minute. Elrod kept peering in the window; when he saw Pine step into the kitchen he followed, coming in three steps behind. They crept down the hall and heard music coming from a room off the hall. Pine eased up outside the open door, and they listened hard. They heard two voices, male and female, though it was unclear what they were saying with the music playing. Pine turned and nodded, holding up three fingers. They both knew the drill: On three, they would enter in stack formation, Pine going right and El left. Each would shoot anyone in their quadrant. Pine closed his fist, third finger gone. They stepped in and fired before Gross or Thomas could make a peep. Pop, pop; one in the chest for each. They moved to either side of the bed and each fired one more round, one behind the ear to make sure. They were out the back door in a flash. The whole thing was over in less than three minutes. They exfiltrated to their car and were gone. Pine drove, as he always did, and Elrod texted Stilton a one-word text. It read "Done." To his surprised, he got an immediate response. It read: "Need one more house painted. Details tomorrow."

Fifty-nine

The following morning the two agents sitting outside Professor Gross's house called Bill Kearney at 8:30. The senior guy, named Dobbs, made the call. Kearney answered as always, "Kearney."

"Sir, Agent Dobbs here; my partner and I are sitting stakeout at the Gross residence. We came on at 3:00 a.m. and relieved the other team. I'm calling because the pattern here is off. Normally the Thomas woman comes over at night and leaves around 6:30. It's 8:30, and we're not seeing any movement over there. I figured I better check with you."

Kearney felt his gut tense, saying, "Did anything odd happen during the night? Anything at all?"

"No, sir. It was quiet; not a creature stirring from 3:00 on. The other agents had nothing to tell. They said she got here around 7:30 and went inside. Nothing since. This feels wrong, sir. I don't like it."

Kearney swore under his breath saying, "Sit tight, Dobbs. We don't want to spook them if they got into the wine and overslept. I'll have someone call and see if they pick up. Don't make a move. And Dobbs, be alert."

"Roger that, sir."

Bill Kearney was concerned. He did not think the Thomas woman knew they were watching, and they had not actively been on Gross. He called Thomas's office and was told she was not there. They were concerned too, having gotten no answer to repeated calls that morning. Now Bill Kearney felt the weight of it settle on his shoulders. He called Winston, gave him a situation report, and asked him to send a car to Gross's place. If anyone answered the door they were to act surprised and ask for a Mrs. Felix. Kearney hoped to Christ that happened, and this turned out to be nothing. It did not turn out to be nothing.

The two patrol cops rolled up to the Gross residence and went to the door. One banged on the door with his duty flashlight, loud enough to wake the dead. His partner walked around the house and saw nothing. There was a car in the driveway, which was the Thomas woman's. They had the plates run, and word came back to Winston, who was by now in Kearney's office. They decided they had no choice; the officers forced entry, and a grim discovery awaited them. They found the dead couple in the first bedroom, deader than stones. The alarm was raised, crime techs were dispatched, and the tedious processing of the crime scene followed. Kearney and Winston showed up a bit later and viewed the grisly scene.

Kearney was beyond angry, saying to Winston, "What the fuck happened? Our guys are good. They swear this Thomas woman had no idea they were on her. Goddamn it, how in blue blazes did this happen?"

"No idea," Winston responded. "But if your guys heard and saw nothing, this was a pro hit. One behind the ear, no one saw or heard shit. I'm thinking the same two dirt balls did the temple massacre."

"Has to be," Kearney said. "But how did anyone know we were looking? I mean, we've been super cautious. I don't understand it, I really don't." Winston had no answer, and the two men left the crime scene team to do their work. They found nothing.

Sixty

Decker sat at an outside table at Rook Coffee Shop on Freret Street. It was 7:15 that morning, two days after the professor and Penelope Thomas were found shot to death. That had really upset the apple cart and set everyone scrambling. It was a mystery, for sure; no one seemed to have even a hint as to how it came about. Decker was deep in thought, wondering if his bump would be enough to shake Jenna Dupreaux into making a foolish move. He was tired; hell, they were all tired. Working long hours and still coming up short. It's a wonderful life, he thought.

Serendipity saved him, just sheer luck. He was lost in thought and failed to notice the man who sat down at the next table. Had he looked, he would have seen a man in a T-shirt and jeans, sunglasses, and a ball cap pulled low. Nothing unusual there, but the man was browned by the sun and had ropey, muscular arms that suggested he was in fine physical condition. A puff of wind, gentle as baby's breath, pushed his napkin off the table. Decker had excellent reflexes and reached to grab it in free fall. As he bent below the tabletop, he glimpsed the boots below the adjacent table. Brown leather, with EL written on the inside of the boot's upper, right above the sole.

A flood of adrenaline hit his system, but he grabbed the napkin and sat upright as though all was well. He took a sip of coffee, stood, and dropped a five on the tabletop. He turned ever so slightly and pulled the brass knuckles from his pocket. He yawned, stretched, and made as if to leave; he walked so that his right side would be near the seated man and his left hand blocked from view.

As he got alongside the man he turned on his right foot, executing a left hook to the side of the man's head. It was a savage blow, and Decker knew this guy was out of the fight. He dropped low, out of sight for a moment. He put the brass knuckles into his pocket and pulled the Glock 30 from the small of his back. He popped his head up and did a quick scan but saw no one else that could be a threat. He rolled the man's body a little and saw an earbud on his other ear. He knew then; the other killer would be in a car parked on the street.

The plan was obvious: This one would pop him once he left the coffee shop. His accomplice would pull up, pick up his buddy, and they would be gone in less than thirty seconds. Only now Decker had other plans.

He looked up and down the street, trying to look casual. But the other man was a pro and saw Decker looking. Not seeing his pal, he hit the start button on the SUV and was trying to pull out of the parallel parking space he was in. Decker saw him halfway down the block and started to sprint. He was fast, in excellent physical condition, and got there just as the SUV started to accelerate rapidly. He saw someone in the driver's seat and could only make out a ball cap.

The SUV leapt forward, and Decker knew this was the guy, putting pedal to the metal. He had to decide: Shoot or play it safe. He feared they would not get another chance like this one. He took a shooter's stance and emptied the clip into the back windshield of the SUV. It crashed twenty yards further down.

Decker popped his empty clip, slammed in a second clip, and started to ease toward the wrecked car. He was wary; he knew he was lucky to still be alive and he wanted to keep it that way. Off in the distance he heard sirens and figured someone had called in shots fired. He used parked cars as cover and waited for backup to arrive, keeping the SUV covered as he tried to slow his breathing.

Four minutes later a cruiser roared up and stopped at the other end of the block. He had called dispatch and told them to tell the cops he was on foot, behind the wrecked car, with a dangerous man inside. He did not want panicked cops shooting him. He poked his head out and waved his shield at the cops.

Slowly they all moved forward. Inside the SUV the driver was slumped over, dead. Several wounds were visible and as the adrenaline spike wore off, Decker slumped to the pavement and propped his back against a car. Sirens filled the air as a host of cop cars swooped in.

Sixty-one

With any police shooting, the area is saturated with cops. The scene on Freret Street was no exception. Cops, crime scene techs, and the media buzzed like flies within a short time after Decker's near brush with death. Decker now sat with Winston and Kearney on a bench near Rook Coffee. They all had a fresh cup in hand, and the captain and Kearney wanted a full rundown on what had happened. Decker walked them through it all, describing his good luck in spotting EL on the boots of the man at Rook. That man had been taken by ambulance to University Hospital and was in surgery. They would learn later that he had a severe concussion and his jaw joint was shattered. When he finished giving them the facts, Decker added, "It's kinda crazy. Why would these guys come after me? I'm just another cog in a big wheel."

Winston then said, "I don't know, either. Maybe you got a little close to the bone with someone and didn't know it. So far we've found two silenced nines, one with the guy you hit and the other in the SUV. The man you hit had a stun gun in one pocket and your picture in the other. It came from the net, an older fight photo. Looks like he planned to zap you in the street, shoot you, and be gone. The partner's gun, the dead guy, was in the floorboard and likely flew off the seat in the crash. We don't have IDs yet, but I'll bet you my eyeteeth ballistics matches slugs from these guns to the Gross shooting."

Bill Kearney chimed in saying, "Yes, that seems likely to me. Decker, when you talked to Roe Stilton, did it get heated?"

"No, I wouldn't say that. I did tweak him a bit, especially about his druggie son. The little bastard is just so arrogant. What a shit he is. Maybe it all tracks back to him; Nazis, the attack, his son, the whole nine yards. Yeah, I could see that. It was like he thought he was a royal and found it demeaning to speak with a commoner who questioned him anyway."

Kearney jumped in. "Yes, that would fit. We often see these top guys are very narcissistic and don't take well to anyone troubling them. Just imperious bastards who think they can bull over anyone and everyone. Money makes it worse, so that could be it. On the other hand, my guys did bump Jenna Dupreaux, and she could have lashed out."

"Nah, it doesn't feel like that. I don't see her in the Nazi temple stuff. She's all about herself. I think if it was her she would have tried to take me down on her own. Maybe seduction and a drug overdose—much more her style."

Winston added, "Well, we may find out more when this EL guy is able to speak. Course, that may be a while. Decker fucked him up pretty good."

"It was just a love tap, Cap," Decker responded.

"Yeah, right; my guys say you could see the marks on the side of his face. Looked a lot like those old school brass knuckles to them. Course, they're illegal, so I'm sure they are mistaken."

"Absolutely, Captain. I would never ..."

"Yeah, yeah, yeah; I feel no sympathy for this mutt. Especially if he's one of the temple shooters. We may never know, though, if he clams up."

Kearney piped up, "He'll talk. May take a bit of work, but he'll roll in the end."

Winston asked, "Why are you so sure, Bill?"

Kearney smiled, saying, "We're in Louisiana. If he buttons up and won't roll, he goes to Angola. If he rolls and spills on the higher-ups, we'll offer him life in Leavenworth. With the temple massacre and the Gross killings, he's toast.

He'll never get out. His choices: three hots and a cot in Leavenworth or he goes to Angola, where he'll take it up the Khyber Pass every day. He won't live a week in Angola. I've got texted photos of him from the hospital. Big swastika on his back and 'No niggers allowed' on his right bicep. He may be dumb, but his lawyer will help him figure this one out." Three weeks later Ricky Elrod cut a deal and named names. His jaw was still wired shut, and his eyes didn't seem to move in sync due to the blow to his head. They had identified J.R. Pine, and both men had extensive backgrounds in special forces and then as contract soldiers with Tidal Basin Security.

Sixty-two

Decker was there to snap the cuffs on Roe Stilton when he was arrested on a multitude of charges. With the help of Ricky Elrod, they found bank transfers to pay for the temple massacre and the hits on Gross and Thomas. There was one more, and Decker knew it was for the botched hit on him. He had requested that he be at the arrest and allowed to cuff Stilton. Winston agreed, and on that Wednesday morning they showed up unannounced at 6:00 at Stilton's house. Stilton came to the door in his pajamas, and when he opened the door Decker snatched him out by the lapels and cuffed him. His pajamas had little hearts all over them, and they almost fell out laughing when they looked down. The little runt was wearing footie pajamas. As he snapped the cuffs on tight, Decker remarked snidely, "Nice pj's, short stuff. Where'd you get those, Midgets R Us?"

Stilton flushed and screamed, "What is the meaning of this? How dare you speak to me that way? I'll have your badge, Detective. Mark my word, you're done."

Decker laughed in his face, saying, "You won't be doing much of anything for a very long time. Ricky Elrod, one of your attack dogs, dimed you out. We got bank transfers, his testimony, lots more. You won't see daylight for the rest of your miserable little life. The rest of your little Nazi band of brothers is being arrested this morning. Want to bet they point a finger at you?"

"You insolent swine. Take your hands off me. You are a mongrel, just like so many others in this city."

"Maybe so, but tonight I'll be sleeping in my bed. My guess is you'll be at New Orleans metro. The gang bangers will love the footie pajamas. You'll have no friends and fine cuisine, my man. Officers, take this man downtown to booking." Stilton was led away and was screaming about his lawyer all the way. Decker felt a measure of satisfaction.

Despite cracking the Chabad-Lubavitch massacre, Decker was still stuck with respect to Jenna Dupreaux. She seemed to have dropped her relationship with Darren Nakot. They both were going about their lives indifferent to the suspicions of the cops. Decker knew, though, that with Jenna, it was only a matter of time. She would eventually do something else given her personality. He'd informed Double L and Captain Crunch of his feelings. They sent him to speak more with the department's shrinks, who listened to his story and filled in as best they could with a profile. Bill Kearney offered to let one of the Behavioral Science Unit do a workup on Jenna in thanks for the good work Decker had done on the temple case. The workup concluded that the subject female was almost certainly a psychopath and therefore a narcissist. It stated that all psychopaths are narcissists, but not all narcissists are psychopaths. It characterized the subject as organized, a meticulous planner, but deep down insecure. Most of all, it highlighted the danger that such a person posed to anyone who stood in the subject's way. Decker believed that and tried to figure a way to use some of this knowledge to his advantage. It was nearly Thanksgiving, and he still was scratching his head. Jenna Dupreaux was enjoying life as a new anchor for WWL in the morning, and he did not like that one bit.

Sixty-three

It was two days before Thanksgiving, cold and wet outside. Jenna sat on her sofa with a glass of wine and her music playing softly. She felt better; things had been quiet for a bit. She had the anchor job, she was boinking Win regularly and might be making an inroad there. Best of all, the damn cops were not hounding her. She was thinking about bed when there was a knock on her door. She glanced at her phone: 11:03. Actually, she thought, it was more than a knock. Someone was banging on her door. She slipped over to the door and peeped out the little spyglass set in the door. It was Crawford Stilton. She knew his father had been arrested earlier, and she heard he was not taking it well. What on earth?

Jenna opened the door. She'd known Crawford for eons and did not think he was capable of violence. She figured he was just high and wandering in the night. Jenna did not want to trifle with Crawford, and when she had the door open she said, "Crawford, what the hell are you doing? It's 11:00 at night. Go home, Crawford." Crawford did not go home; he shoved his way in and slammed the door behind him. Jenna could see from his pupils he was high, and she stepped back a half step. Crawford leered at her, saying, "I want some pussy, Jenna."

Jenna could hardly believe her ears. The nerve of this little bastard. He was no taller than she was, and she wanted to break open his head. She responded, "You twit. Get out of my house, now. You're high, and I'll call the cops, Crawford. I'm in no mood to put up with your shit."

Crawford smiled a loopy smile, saying, "Yeah, Jenna, call the cops. I'll wait right here for 'em. See, I got a story to tell. I figured it out."

"Figured out what, you moron? There's nothing to figure out." Even as she spoke, Jenna felt a chill down her spine.

"Oh, there's a lot to tell. See, my dealer knows your fuck buddy Dare. He tells me Dare supplies all the fentanyl that's on the street. I put it together: you, Dare, fentanyl, and Alisha Bondurant. You killed Alisha. Dare supplied the drugs, and you did the deed. Think the cops will be interested in those facts, Jenna?" Crawford said, leering again.

Jenna tried a bluff, saying, "Ridiculous. Who would ever believe such a fairy story? Now go, Crawford. I'm serious." Crawford rocked a bit on his feet and then said, "Nah, I think I'll have a blow job instead. Call the cops, Jenna. I'm not leaving." Jenna felt danger rush upon her. She knew if Decker and the cops got wind of this she could be in for a time of it. She was also concerned that Dare might spill the beans if Crawford got him jammed up. She decided to play for time, think on it and said, "Okay, Crawford, come in. Have a drink, and we'll talk it out."

Crawford was not having any of it, saying, "Jenna, get naked right now or call the cops. If you don't, I'm calling 911. It's a fucking emergency," and almost choked he was laughing so hard at his own joke.

Jenna thought, "Fuck all, I need to be rid of him and Dare." Just like that, a plan came to her. She changed her tone, saying, "Okay, Crawford, you are kinda cute. Let's go get a little blow to spice things up. Come on, I need to change. You can watch." She headed for her bedroom, and Crawford followed. Jenna yanked the nightgown over her head and dropped it to the floor. She did a full 360 degree turn, and she knew then she had him. Jenna got a little aroused thinking about what was to come. She got dressed in black pants, black top, black boots, and scarf. She made sure to put on gloves and even added a dark baseball cap to her ensemble. She made sure to bend over and give him a few tantalizing looks. Crawford was putty in her hands. She thought she could have put on a bearskin rug with the head on top and he would not have noticed. Finished, she said, "Let's go over to Dare's. We'll get the coke, come back here, and I'll fuck your wisdom teeth loose. Let's take your car. It's in my drive, right?"

"Yeah, sure. We can do that. You drive; I'm a little wasted. Don't need a cop stop. Not tonight."

Jenna made sure to give him a kiss on the lips and lean in, pressing hard against him. She led him out to the car, and they headed for Dare's place. Jenna drove and kept up the seductive routine, not letting Crawford's mind leave sex. They drove over and knocked on Dare's door. It was now 11:35, and Jenna saw no one in the parking lot of Dare's condominium. Dare came to the door, seeing Jenna first and then Crawford. He said, "Jenna, who's this guy? What do you want?"

Jenna smiled sweetly, saying, "Let us in. He's an old school friend. I just want to buy a little blow. Then we'll be gone." Dare was a bit suspicious, but figured, "Okay, sell the blow and get them out of here ASAP." They went inside, and Dare pointed to his kitchen table. They sat, and he went to the back to get his stash. In a minute he was back and took a chair at the table with them. He had a scale and a bag of dope, and he measured some out. Crawford slapped a hundred on the table, and Dare added to the scale. Jenna said, "I've got to go powder my nose. You two get acquainted." She went back to Dare's bedroom and found the little .25 she had returned after the Hunter business. She closed the bathroom door and checked the clip; one in the chamber and three in the clip. Perfect. She held the little gun slightly behind her and walked back to the kitchen. Dare was still sitting, fiddling with the scales. Crawford had a line of blow on the table and was picking up a straw. Jenna leaned down, slipped her arms under Dare's armpits, and acted as if she was going to hug him. Instead she slid the muzzle up under his chin and pulled the trigger, ducking her head slightly. Pop, but not so loud. Little gun, contact wound, flesh and mouth cavity caught the noise. The little .25 round likely did the tour in Dare's head but did not come out the top. Crawford, just finishing the line, looked up dumbly saying, "Wha ..." She shot him twice in the chest, pop, pop; no muss, no fuss. She moved quickly, grabbing a couple of paper towels from the roll. She wiped the gun down and then put it in Dare's limp hand, making sure there were prints on the gun. She tried to decide what to do with his arm and the gun and finally just used his hand to pick the little gun up, bring it toward his chin, and let it go. The gun clattered to the floor, and his arm fell off to the side. She put that towel in her pocket. She thought hard: Had she touched anything? Maybe the dresser drawer knob where he kept the gun and the bathroom door. She wiped them with the second towel, went to the front door, cracked it an inch. No sound, just rain pattering. No one moving; everything still. She pulled the door closed with the second towel and pocketed it. She walked home in the rain whistling "My Fair Lady."

Sixty-four

By Thanksgiving the bodies had been discovered. A neighbor complained of the smell and noted Dare's car had not moved in several days. Decker heard about it when Gail Waites phoned him. She said, "Darren Nakot is dead. So is some other White dude, name of Crawford Stilton. Thought you'd want to know."

Decker felt like a mule had kicked him in the gut. "What, wait, Gail ... what the hell are you talking about?"

Gail replied, "Yep, no doubt about it. My guy in narcotics called me. When they went in they found a pile of blow and two dead bodies. Called the narc squad, and my friend Dre responded. He says Darren had a contact wound under his chin. Other dude took two right in the chest. Little .25 on the floor. Been there a couple days. Smell tipped it off."

"Ahh, fuck. Fuck me. I can't believe it. This can't be right."

"Go see for yourself. Dre's still there. I'll tell him you're coming. Okay?" Gail said.

"Yeah, thanks, I know where Darren lives. Charlotte Commons Condominiums. I'll talk to you when I know more." Decker nearly slammed his phone down in frustration. He hurried out to the Mustang and sped off to Darren's condo. He arrived to find blue flashing lights and crime scene tape. He pulled a lanyard with his shield over his neck and hustled over. He got by the patrol cops, but a Black guy in a suit stopped him.

"Hold up, man. Are you Decker?" the Black man asked.

"Yeah, you must be Dre. Gail called you, right?"

"She did. Slow down, man, crime scene guys in there working. Don't want your hoof prints all over the place. Let me give you the skinny. Just like I told Gail. This Darren dude must have shot this other Stilton dude. Stilton has a double tap to the chest. Blow on the table. Darren Nakot slumped in a chair with a scale and a bag of blow in front of him. A little .25 caliber on the floor. Looks like a murder suicide, got to be. But here's what bugs me. I picked up the gun with gloves on. Still one in the chamber. It holds six in the clip; three shots fired here. One in the chamber. Where the other two?"

Decker squeezed his eyes shut and wiped his hand over his face. He thought a moment, then said, "I suspect there was a third person. The shooter. Shit, I cannot believe it. Goddamn it."

"How you figure that, man? Nakot shot under the chin. Two in the other dude's chest. No evidence anybody else was around. I guess we'll see what the crime scene guys pull, but it looks pretty much like I told you. We'll talk to the neighbors, look for cameras; there'll be an autopsy, all that stuff. I'll keep you posted, man. If you want, wait for a while, and then you can go in when the tech guys finish."

Decker said, "They won't find anything. Guarantee it. The chick that killed these guys is way too smart to leave a trail."

"Man, you gotta be trippin'. No offense, but this Stilton dude's car is parked in the lot and the door was locked from the inside. I cain't see it, no offense."

"None taken," Decker replied. "I wouldn't buy it if I were in your shoes either. But I know. I feel it in my bones. Goddamn it." Decker waited until they let him in; the scene was just as Dre described. Nice and neat; the only oddity was the one bullet still in the chamber. Decker had a pretty good idea where the other two bullets were. Wherever poor Sue Hunter's body was, that would be where the other two slugs were. He knew it as surely as he knew his own name. But once again, he feared Jenna would skate. They'd wait for forensics, but he was not hopeful. His fears were confirmed as the results of the crime scene analysis and ballistics rolled in. No evidence of a third party involved in the shooting, and it went in the books as a murder suicide. Decker knew in his heart that was bullshit.

Sixty-five

It was Thanksgiving in New Orleans. The Waltons always invited guests to their house the Friday night after Thanksgiving. People dropped in and out, chatted, socialized, and left. Just a loose gathering of old friends and their kids. The crowd swelled and dwindled as folks came and went. It was a well-heeled crowd, as Mr. Walton was a banker and had lots of wealthy friends and clients. It was a tradition that had stood for many years. Jenna had Win in tow, and they came for drinks, seeing friends and catching up. Jenna felt terrific, on top of her game. The Nakot murder suicide had filled the society pages and made big news in New Orleans. The cops said it was a drug deal gone bad, a murder suicide. Jenna had attended both funerals, dressed appropriately and weeping to show her sorrow. They had brought Roe Stilton in manacles to the graveside, and Jenna hugged him for show. To all the world, Jenna was as shocked and sorry as anyone that the senseless deaths had occurred.

Decker watched both services and felt White hot anger blossom in his chest as she put on a show. He was sure Jenna was the killer, but he had no evidence. Damn it to hell, she was slick. He had to give her that. He knew putting her away was going to be the biggest challenge of his career, maybe the biggest for his entire career. People just did not see a smiling twenty-two-year-old White girl as a killer. She was from money, her heritage was good, and she was an anchor on the news. No, to the outside world Jenna Dupreaux was above suspicion. Decker had a lot of leeway with his bosses, the temple case having upped his stock. After the second funeral, Decker met Gail Waites at a fast-food joint not far from the cemetery. He laid it all out for Gail, who listened intently. When he was done, Gail asked, "Decker, do you think Dare killed Anita? If you right, this White girl is a maniac, killing all these people. I know Dare sold drugs and did lots of women, but nothing in his past showed any violence. Makes we wonder, ya know?"

"Yeah, I do know. Gail, we may never know. Probably won't, because I don't think Jenna will crack, even if we get her down the road. I'm at my wit's end; I cannot catch this girl, and I'm not sure I ever will. She is as slick as any killer could ever be. Plus, look at her. Nobody sees a killer except me. I feel it; hell, I know it. But I can't prove she spit on the sidewalk. I need a way in, that's what I need."

Gail ate a couple of fries and said, "Decker, you goin' at this all wrong. This girl is used to getting what she wants, all day every day. You told me she's a narcissist. Play to that. You a good-lookin' guy. See if you can use her narcissism against her. Women do not like to be put down by men they are attracted to. I know; I deal with women and sex crimes every day. Think on it. I gotta roll. Catch you later." Gail left and Decker thought, "Yeah, maybe. Better than I've got now." He got in the Mustang and headed for home. Over the next couple of weeks a plan started to form in his mind. He worked it around, looked at the angles. It might work.

Sixty-six

Gail was drinking heavily as Christmas approached. She saw lives shattered every day in her job. She felt the enormous loss of Anita, and she shared the pain with Jean as best she could. Jean was a shell of her former self. The death of Anita had killed Jean just as surely as if she had been given a dose of slow-acting poison. It might be years, but Jean would die broken and hollow. Gail would too; they were born into poverty and misery and would almost certainly die in misery over their loss. Gail had seen lots of violence in her youth and witnessed the carnage of the sex crimes she investigated. Gail had been sure Darren Nakot had killed Anita; Jean still thought so. But Gail knew that if he did it was almost certainly an accident. The man was a lowlife piece of scum, but he was not known to be violent. It did not quite fit. On the other hand, if Decker was right, this society bitch was a serial killer. Gail wondered if she had a hand in Anita's death. Darren was now dead, and Gail had expected his death to bring some peace to her and Jean. It did not happen. They still were in the dark on what actually happened with Anita. More importantly, nothing would bring her back. The hole in their heart hurt every single day. Now Decker was suffering from depression and anger over Jenna Dupreaux. Gail thought maybe a bit of street justice was in order. She'd have to think it through, but maybe.

Decker was in fact struggling. At the Resolve gym they had banned him from sparring, saying he was too brutal and hurting the other fighters. He was down twelve pounds from 190, only a few pounds over his fighting weight of 175. He was cut, strong, and angry. He beat the heavy bag with a fierceness that made folks keep some distance. Everyone told him he needed to relax. Thing was, he could not relax. He kept hearing bump, bump, bump in his mind, and his thoughts ran to Jenna and dead bodies. He awoke in a sweat nightly, the dream always the same. The Hunter woman imploring him to find her killer and do justice.

Christmas came and went, and Decker set his plan in motion. He followed Jenna until she went into The Pressed Grape. He came in a few minutes later and found her at the bar, with a glass of merlot. She smiled brightly at him, saying, "Why Decker? What brings you into my territory?"

Decker said, "Jenna, I know you killed Alisha. I know you killed the Hunter woman, Darren Nakot, and the Stilton kid too. I see right through your veneer."

Jenna laughed a challenging laugh, saying, "You need a drink. I'll buy, what are you having?" She motioned over the server and ordered Decker a specialty beer. She continued, "Decker, really. That is so absurd I'm going to forget it. We could be friends, you know. I could do my hair in pigs, let you pull on them while you, ah ... do me from behind. Yeah, that sounds right. Kinda makes me hot, you know?"

Decker knew the moment was right. He gave her the predator smile and stunned her by saying, "Jenna, I wouldn't fuck you with someone else's dick. I don't do retreads. Have a happy New Year." He stood and walked out, never looking back. If he had, he would have seen the look in Jenna's eyes. They were the eyes of a killer, cold, black, anger flashing and her brain screamed, "Kill that son of bitch right now." But Jenna knew she would not, at least not right at that moment. She would plan and take her time. But he was dead, no ifs, ands, or buts. That son of a bitch was a dead man walking.

Decker had played his role well. He headed for home and called Double L on the way. Captain Winston was in the loop, and they would set up on Decker's house for the next few days. The New Year was a couple days off, and they felt that given his slight, Jenna would make a move to kill Decker within the next three or four days. The profilers and shrinks agreed: Her ego could not take that kind of bashing without lashing out. Decker was the goat, tethered to a tree. Now they waited to see if the lioness was taking the bait.

Sixty-seven

Decker paced around his house and went about his business as the New Year rolled in. The watchers covered him twenty-four hours a day for the next four days. But nothing happened. They were all keyed up and ready to react, but it was crickets. On the first work day of the New Year Decker was at this desk drinking coffee when Captain Winston called. He said, "You sitting down?"

"Yes, sir. What's up?"

Winston replied, "I just heard over the news that Jenna Dupreaux was found this morning shot to death in her house. Can you believe that?"

Decker nearly choked, as coffee went down the wrong way and he fell into a coughing fit. Finally it ended, he could hear Winston saying, "You okay? Decker? Hey man, talk to me. Otherwise, I'm calling the paramedics."

Decker finally gasped, "No, no ... I just let coffee go down my windpipe. I'm fine. Christ, are you serious? What in the world is going on? I just knew she would come after me. I was sure of it. The shrinks were too. Now, you're telling me she's dead. Gunshots? Are they sure it was not a suicide?"

"Not unless she shot herself twice in the chest and then behind the ear and walked off with the gun. You'd have been a suspect but our guys were on you like White on rice. But somebody got to her. She's gone."

Decker slumped back in his chair. Never in his wildest dreams had he expected that. He was dumbstruck, not knowing what to think. He followed up with the crime scene folks and tried to get some idea of who had killed Jenna. He wondered about Gail, but this was so much like

Jenna's murders. Planned, executed to perfection, and no one knew or heard anything. Just a big freaking mystery. He went to her funeral but did not go to the cemetery. A day or so later he met Gail for coffee. Gail denied knowing anything, claiming she and Jean learned of the death via the news. Crime scene techs turned up nothing, and all Decker could do was wonder. What in God's name had happened? He felt in his heart they would never know. But one thing was certain: Jenna Dupreaux would not take another life.

Sixty-eight

The killer was satisfied. Not content, but satisfied. It had been a good plan, executed well. The killer had made a modeling clay impression of Jenna's house key at Thanksgiving. Opportunity presented itself, and the doing was easy. A bit of clay, Jenna's purse unattended. The killer had taken it in the bathroom, made an impression, washed the key off, and put the purse back. No one was the wiser, and no one saw or heard anything. They were otherwise occupied. The killer had a .22 revolver; it was an inherited gun, one of several. It was well-preserved and worked perfectly. The killer made sure with target practice regularly over a number of months. The killer waited, watched, and made certain the plan was airtight. It had to work, or the killer would commit suicide. On the night of the murder, the killer slipped quietly into Jenna's house with the key. The killer wore all black, even having a black hoodie purchased from a Walmart. The killer stood patiently in the dark for hours, waiting. Time meant nothing; this was a mission, just like Jenna's missions. There was a target, an enemy who must die. It was only justice. When Jenna came in that evening at 10:07, she snapped on the lights and closed the door, turning the dead bolt. She turned to head toward her shower and the killer stepped out, shooting her twice in the chest. To be sure, the killer put one round behind Jenna's ear. The killer had done research at the library and wanted to do it right. When the act was done, the killer turned off the lights and slipped away into the night. No trace evidence to find. No shell casings since the gun was a revolver. No prints; the killer wore cheap cotton gardening gloves. The gun went into Lake Pontchartrain and would never be found. Now the killer sat watching rain smash on the big window looking out on the lake.

Now it was 2:00 a.m. and the killer was alone in the big house, sipping a glass of port. "I may go to hell for killing Jenna Dupreaux," thought Aline Bondurant. "If I do, so be it. But that bitch is there now, ahead of me, suffering. Happy Fucking New Year!"

EPILOGUE

It was Friday afternoon, two weeks after Jenna was found dead. Decker finished late and headed for Resolve to unwind with some bag work and a bit of sparring if he could find a partner. He arrived at dusk, went in, and found his buddy Danny Ruiz, a gifted middleweight fighter working the speed bag. He walked over and said, "Feel like an ass whipping tonight?"

Ruiz flashed a big grin and retorted, "A slow Paddy dude like you won't lay a glove on me. Be like takin' candy from a baby."

"Excellent," Decker said. "Let me warm up a bit and hit the heavy bag a few. Then we'll go a couple, see what your Mexican ass is made of." Decker changed, gloved up, and went to work. Danny finished his session and moved to the jump rope. Decker had to admire Ruiz; the dude was cat-quick and jumped rope so fast and lightly that it was a thing of beauty to watch. Half an hour later they took a water break and Ruiz taunted, "You ready for that lesson, White boy?"

Decker laughed and said, "Yeah, I might just knock the beans right out of you. You'll be too sore to go see your mami tonight. Tighten your jockstrap, amigo."

They had done this many times and fell into an easy rhythm, first working on defense. One would be the aggressor while the other would play defense, boxing style: parrying, rolling, ducking, the whole bit. They switched roles frequently to keep it fresh. Decker had to admit Ruiz was quicker than a hiccup; he was really hard to land any solid punches on. They did the final round really sparring, although they were not trying for a knockout. They worked on technique and each gave a good showing. Both men were dripping with sweat and glad to be finished when they quit. Ruiz, as always, had something to say, "Man, you hit nothing but my smoke tonight. I owned your White boy ass."

Decker grinned and fired back, "Yeah, I guess that's why you had to pick your mouthpiece up off the mat after that last exchange."

"Bullshit, man. I spit that thing out after we were done." They both started laughing at that one and headed for the shower. Decker showered, cooled under a fan for a few minutes, and dressed. He felt good, satisfied with his workout. Danny was still talking to another fighter when Decker stepped out into the dark. It was January, raw and blowing off the water. He headed for the Scalded Dog, thinking he would be glad to get out of the wind. He'd parked closer to the street; the gym had been humming when he got there. The Scalded Dog had no electronic locks, being a vintage '65 Mustang. He fished the key from his pocket and stepped to the door, key extended. He had some light from a streetlight, and he knew he was on target, but the key would not go in the keyhole. What now, he thought, and never heard the sound of the figure approaching his back. He bent toward the keyhole, saw a paper clip jammed in his door lock, and was hit by a bolt of electricity that shorted out his circuits. He dropped like a stone, never seeing the figure extend a stun gun and push it into his exposed neck.

The Black man saw Decker emerge from the gym. He was parked about twenty feet from Decker's Mustang, with all his lights off and sitting in the cold. As Black as he was, it was virtually impossible to see him through the tinted windows of his Kia. He watched Decker approach his car, pulling his keys from his pocket. The watcher saw a thin figure wearing a ball cap and scarf pulled up to the nose step out from behind a van parked two spaces from the Mustang. The figure was moving way too quickly, and the watcher popped his door and was out in a flash. He saw the figure come up behind Decker and saw a flash of electricity at the back of Decker's head. Shit, he thought, stun gun. He was already drawing his gun and moved into a firing position as he had done many times on the practice range. He saw a glint as the lithe attacker pulled something from a jacket pocket, and he thought "Knife" and fired two rounds at the attacker's back: boom, boom. The attacker pitched forward on top of Decker, who was not moving. The Black man sprinted to the fallen bodies and kicked the figure he had shot, hard. He got no response but did not holster his weapon. He grabbed the figure with his other hand and dragged it off Decker, keeping the gun aimed and ready. Blood was everywhere, and Decker was stirring, slowly. The watcher put a finger to the neck of the person he'd shot and felt no pulse. He looked for the knife and saw it had bounced a few feet away. He stepped to it and saw that it was an eight-inch butcher knife. He kicked it soccer style another fifteen feet and bent to Decker. He yelled, "Hey, man, you all right? Talk to me."

Decker struggled to a sitting position and finally said, "What the fuck happened?"

The shooter said, "Take it easy for a minute, Decker. I gotta call this in. He punched in a number on speed dial and said, "Shots fired. Resolve Gym, Rendon Street. One down; officer needs assistance. Get some cars rolling right the fuck now. And a bus; one down with gunshot wounds."

Decker was examining himself and other than scrapes from the fall onto the pavement, seemed intact. He asked, "Who are you? And who the fuck is that? Man, I feel like somebody stuck a live power line to my neck."

"I'm Dre, Gail's friend in narcotics. We've been taking turns following you since Jenna's death when we could. I caught tonight's shift, lucky for you. Gail just felt this thing was not over."

"Shit. I had no idea. Never saw you or Gail. Nor this asshole, for that matter. I got blood all over me, but I don't feel any wounds. Who is that? And what the hell happened?"

Dre said, "Let's wait for the blues and the ME. I want the scene just as it is since I did the shooting. Knife over there where I kicked it; eight-inch butcher knife. I think the perp is dead. I felt no pulse. I saw you come out, try to get in your car. Saw the perp start for you and drew my weapon. When I saw the blue flash at the back of your head, I knew it was not good. I saw a glint as the perp pulled something from a jacket pocket. I fired twice, at the center of the back. Perp fell on you, and here we are. I'm betting that knife is sharp and has a nasty point. Don't think this was a social event with cheese slices. I think you were about to test that blade for sharpness."

"No doubt. I'd be dead without your help. Thanks, man ... uh, Dre. Man, I feel lightheaded."

"Adrenaline spike; it'll burn off soon. Sit still."

An hour later Decker was drinking a cup of coffee and wrapped in a blanket, leaning against a black and white. Gail had shown up, and Dre was still giving a statement. Gail said, "Hard to believe. That's Suzanne Dupreaux, Jenna's mother. Looks like she wanted to end your run right here in this parking lot."

Decker shook his head, saying, "You know what they say: Like mother, like daughter. Damn, just damn. Thanks, Gail. Somewhere in all this mess, Anita got a measure of justice."

Gail nodded. "Won't bring her back, but I think you're right about that. Only in New Orleans. Voodoo and witchcraft trump logic and reason every time."

About the Author

Jeff Head is a lawyer practicing in Mobile, Alabama. He is a graduate of the University of Georgia, Cumberland School of Law and New York University. He is an avid reader and fan of crime fiction, and a true crime buff. He is interested in many sports, and has taken up boxing at age 68 to get fitter and fight complacency. An avid fan of Georgia football, he has written *I'm a Dawg, You're a Dawg and We All Picked Up Some Fleas in Athens*. Head lives with his wife, Luvie, and takes donuts to his granddaughters most Saturdays in the fall. To this point in his life, no one has been able to knock any sense into him.

About the Publisher

The Sager Group was founded in 1984. In 2012 it was chartered as a multimedia content brand, with the intent of empowering those who create art—an umbrella beneath which makers can pursue, and profit from, their craft directly, without gatekeepers. TSG publishes books; ministers to artists and provides modest grants; and produces documentary, feature, and commercial films. By harnessing the means of production, The Sager Group helps artists help themselves. For more information, please see www. TheSagerGroup.net.

More Books from The Sager Group

The Swamp: Deceit and Corruption in the CIA
An Elizabeth Petrov Thriller (Book 1)
by Jeff Grant

Chains of Nobility: Brotherhood of the Mamluks (Books 1-3)
by Brad Graft

Meeting Mozart: A Novel Drawn from the Secret Diaries
of Lorenzo Da Ponte
by Howard Jay Smith

Death Came Swiftly: A Novel About the Tay Bridge Disaster of 1879
by Bill Abrams

A Boy and His Dog in Hell: And Other Stories
by Mike Sager

Reunion in Paradise: A Novel
by L.W. Harris
c*The Orphan's Daughter: A Novel*
by Jan Cherubin

Lifeboat No. 8: Surviving the Titanic
by Elizabeth Kaye

Into the River of Angels: A Novel
by George R. Wolfe

The Dreyfus Collection: A Novel
by Estelle Rubin Brager

See our entire library at TheSagerGroup.net

THE SAGER GROUP
Artifex Te Adiuva